Enchanting
Sebastian

A Big Sky Royal Novel

New York Times & USA Today Bestselling Author
KRISTEN PROBY

ENCHANTING SEBASTIAN

A Big Sky Royal Novel

Kristen Proby

Copyright © 2019 by Kristen Proby

Cover Design: By Hang Le

Formatting: Uplifting Author Services

Cover photo: Perrywinkle Photography

Published by Ampersand Publishing, Inc.

&
AMPERSAND
PUBLISHING, INC.

Glossary

Please know this may contain spoilers for anyone new to the series. The books each couple stars in is noted next to their description.

The King Family:

Jeff and Nancy King – Retired owners of the Lazy K Ranch. Parents of Josh and Zack King.

Josh King – Partner of Lazy K Ranch. Married to Cara Donovan. {Loving Cara}

Zack King – Partner of Lazy K Ranch. Married to Jillian Sullivan (Jillian is the sister of Ty Sullivan). Parents to Seth, Miles and Sarah. {Falling for Jillian}

Doug and Susan King – Doug is Jeff's brother. They live mostly in Arizona, but come to Montana in the summer. Parents of Noah and Grayson.

Noah King – Owner of Wild Wings Bird Sanctuary. Married to Fallon McCarthy, a yoga instructor and owner of Asana Yoga Studio. {Soaring With Fallon}

Grayson King – Ski Instructor on Whitetail Ski Resort. Married to Autumn O'Dea, a Pop music sensation. {Hold On, A Crossover Novella by Samantha Young}

The Sullivan Family:

Ty Sullivan – Attorney. Brother of Jillian. Married to Lauren Cunningham, a bestselling author, whose great grandfather first settled Cunningham Falls. Parents to Layla. {Seducing Lauren}

The Hull Family:

Brad Hull – Chief of Police. Married to Hannah Malone, an OB/GYN. {Charming Hannah}

Jenna Hull – Owner of Snow Wolf Lodge. Married to actor and superstar, Christian Wolfe. {Kissing Jenna}

Max Hull – Self-made billionaire. Married to Willa Monroe (Sister to Jesse Anderson), owner of Dress It Up. Parents to Alex Monroe. {Waiting for Willa}

The Henderson Family:

Brooke Henderson – Owner of Brooke's Blooms. Married to Brody Chabot, architect. {Tempting Brooke, a 1001 Dark Nights Novella}

Maisey Henderson – Owner of Cake Nation. Married to Tucker McCloud, pro football player. {Nothing Without You, A Crossover Novella by Monica Murphy}

The Royal Family:

Prince Sebastian Wakefield – The Duke of Somerset. Married to Nina Wolfe (sister to Christian). {Enchanting Sebastian}

Prince Frederick Wakefield – Brother to Sebastian. Married to Catherine. No book belongs to this couple, as they are already married when introduced.

Prince Callum – Brother to Sebastian.

Princess Eleanor – Sister to Sebastian.

Jacob Baxter – Sebastian's best friend. Owner of Whitetail Mountain, along with several local businesses, including the restaurant Ciao. Married to Grace Douglas.

Liam Cunningham – Head of Montana security, and personal bodyguard to Sebastian. Cousin to Lauren Cunningham.

Nick Ferguson – Personal bodyguard to Nina Wolfe.

Miscellaneous and important characters:

Jesse Anderson - Former Navy deep-sea diver. Married to Tara Hunter. {Worth Fighting For, A Crossover Collection Novella by Laura Kaye}

Joslyn Meyers – Pop star. Married to Kynan McGrath. {Wicked Force, A Crossover Collection Novella by Sawyer Bennett}

Dr. Drake Merritt – Surgeon. Married to Abigail Darwin. Both characters are best friends of Hannah Malone. {Crazy Imperfect Love, A Crossover Collection Novella by K. L. Grayson}

Penelope (Penny) – Former teacher. Married to Trevor Wood, Drummer for the rock band, Adrenaline. {All Stars Fall, A Crossover Collection Novella by Rachel Van Dyken}

Aspen Calhoun – New owner of Drips & Sips.

Sam Waters – EMT.

Note from the Author

Dear Reader,

I don't know about you, but I've been in love with the royal family since I was a small girl, and I woke up in the middle of the night to watch Princess Diana marry Prince Charles with my mother. Everything about that wedding enthralled me, and I can honestly say, I've never missed a televised royal wedding since that day.

I've wanted to write a royal book for a long time, but it always seemed intimidating to me. And then Prince Sebastian took up residence in my head, and he just would not shut up.

Bringing royals to Big Sky was a great joy for me. Sebastian and Nina's story is, of course, a work of fiction. I took many liberties with the royal family, so much so that what I've written is *not* at all how the real royal family works. At least, not to my knowledge.

Then again, I don't spend any time with the monarchy.

This is one hundred percent my take on the *what ifs* of the royal family. Nothing more. So, sit back, put your feet up, grab yourself a snack, and let me tell you a fairy tale…

xoxo,

Kristen

Enchanting Sebastian

A Big Sky Royal Novel

PROLOGUE

Sebastian

"RUNNING AWAY WON'T change anything."

"I'm not running away."

I'm running. Mum isn't wrong. I'm a few months away from my thirty-fifth birthday, unwed, and on the precipice of having a marriage arranged for me, thanks to British law.

I'm the heir to the throne.

I need to be married by thirty-five, or a suitable wife will be found for me.

It's bloody ridiculous.

"Sebastian, you have duties—"

"I love you, Mum. And trust me when I say, I'm well aware of my duty. It's been drilled into me since I was in nappies. I'm not running, I'm taking a holiday."

"How long will you be gone?"

"I don't know."

"Sebastian."

I turn to find my mother's disapproving gaze on me. As the Queen,, my mother is stern, regal, and formal.

But in private, she's kind, happy, and an amazing mum. Her four children adore her.

"Your father will be livid if you leave the country now."

"Father is usually angry about something."

Stiff, distant, and imposing, the king is a force to be reckoned with; it doesn't matter whether you're a member of state or his child.

I respect him as my king, but as a father…I barely know him.

"At least tell me what your plans are," Mum says, laying her hand on my arm. "Tell me you'll be home by your birthday."

"I will," I assure her. "And I'll be married."

"*Sebastian.*"

"I will not have my wife chosen for me. I don't care what the law says."

"If you marry someone who is not a citizen—"

"I'll have to abdicate," I finish for her. As the eldest son of a king, I've been groomed to take over the throne. But I don't want it.

I never did.

"We need to discuss this."

"There's nothing to discuss." I set my bag aside and place my hands on her shoulders, smiling down at her gently. "I love you, Mum. Everything's going to be fine, I promise."

"Tell me where you're going."

"Montana."

She gapes at me. "The United States?"

"That's where Montana is, yes."

"You just returned from there."

"Several months ago," I remind her. "I've always been the traveler of the family. This isn't really that unusual for me."

"Oh, Sebastian. I hope you know what you're doing."

I kiss her cheek, pick up my bag, and walk out of my flat in the palace, heading down the hall in the direction of where a car is waiting to take me to my plane.

I hope I know what I'm doing, as well.

CHAPTER 1

Nina

"I'M NEVER GETTING married."

Silence. I'm sitting at a table with three of my closest friends, and all I get for my announcement is blank stares.

"Never say never," Jenna says. "I didn't think I'd get married either."

"Same," Willa adds and sips her coffee.

"You've been married *twice*," I remind her.

"I'm just saying," Willa continues, "that after my first husband was killed, I didn't think I'd ever get married again."

"I definitely didn't plan to get married," Fallon agrees. "But then I met Noah, and have you *seen* him?"

I sit and stare at my friends. Jenna's married to my brother, making her my sister-in-law. And despite the fact that I initially—and erroneously—thought she wasn't right for him, she's the best ever. I can't imagine our lives without her.

Willa is married to Jenna's brother, Max.

As my yoga instructor, I see Fallon more than anyone else, and she's quickly become one of my closest friends.

We're just one big—*very big*—happy family.

"Why don't you think you'll get married?" Jenna asks before taking a bite of a delicious huckleberry scone. I know it's delicious because I just devoured one myself and am thinking about going back for another.

Drips & Sips does two things very well: coffee and scones.

"It's just a lot of pomp and circumstance for a legal contract. Also, what if it turns out he's an asshole? Or he can't stand me? Then we have to pay a bunch of money for a divorce. It all just sounds expensive and annoying."

"You're such a romantic," Willa says with a snort.

"I'm really not," I say, shaking my head. "I know most girls love the romance stuff. But not me."

"You *don't* like it when a man brings you flowers?" Jenna demands.

"Or surprises you with fun things?" Willa adds.

"Or, you know, has sweet, slow sex with you?" Fallon asks.

I wouldn't know.

No one's ever done those things for me.

And I've done just fine without them in my thirty-one years on this planet, thank you very much.

"It's all a front," I say at last. "It's window coverings. I just want to get to the nitty-gritty and then get on with my life."

"So not a romantic," Willa mutters and finishes her coffee. "And that's okay. Not everyone is. But you never know, someone might eventually come along and give you butterflies and thoughts of happily ever after."

I cock an eyebrow. "I doubt it."

"She's a lost cause when it comes to love," Jenna informs her. "But that's okay. We'll keep her around."

"Thanks." I laugh and decide to forgo the extra scone. I've been slacking on the exercise front and need to get myself under control. "What are you guys up to the rest of the day?"

"I open the shop in about thirty minutes," Willa says, checking the time. "I got some fun new dresses in. You should come and check them out."

Willa owns Dress It Up, a fantastic clothing boutique in downtown Cunningham Falls. It's one of the best stores I've been in, and I've shopped on Rodeo Drive.

"I'll definitely come in. What about you, Jenna?"

"I'm working, too. I have guests coming into the treehouses today, so I need to meet them. And I have another rental to schedule a cleaning for."

"I have a class in thirty minutes," Fallon says. "What about you, Nina? How is the new business going?"

Now butterflies *do* set up residence in my belly. I've been talking about this business for months, and I'm hopeful it'll be off the ground by the end of October.

It's coming up fast. We're already into September.

"It's going well," I reply with a nod. If I could get my supposed partners to call me back, it would be even better. But I don't mention that little snafu. "I'm hoping to launch around Halloween."

"Perfect. Just in time for the holidays," Willa says with a smile. "Keep us posted."

"Oh, I will."

Except, I won't. Because I just don't confide in

people like the others do. Not because I don't care about my friends or trust them. I've just learned to keep my mouth shut.

Having a super celebrity as a brother, and being his manager and publicist, will do that to a girl.

Once we each finish our coffee, the other girls leave, presumably off to get to work. I make a pit stop in the restroom, wave to the barista behind the counter, and push through the glass door.

Plowing right into a hard chest.

"Easy there." Strong arms steady me, and I lean back to look into the bluest eyes I've ever seen.

I know exactly whom they belong to.

"You're like running into a brick wall," I inform Sebastian Wakefield as I step away. We've never formally met, but every woman in the modern world knows who Prince Sebastian is, and I've seen him around town before. "A very pretty brick wall."

"Excuse me," he says formally. "Are you all right, then?"

With a sexy accent to match his sexy face.

"I'm fine. Sorry about that."

I turn to walk away, but he calls after me, "Wait, I think I need your name and number."

I turn and cock an eyebrow. "Why?"

"In case I have any damages later. Trauma." He

grins, and I can see he's teasing me. Maybe even flirting.

It's not every day a real-life prince flirts with a girl.

"We wouldn't want you to have any trauma," I say and give him my sweetest smile. "That would just be horrible for you. You might need comforting."

"My thoughts exactly." His shoulders relax as he retrieves his phone from his pocket.

"Of course, I'd never give my number to a stranger."

His head pops up at that, and he frowns at me. "I beg your pardon?"

"Oh, I'm sure it's unusual for you, as a prince, to be told no. But that's what I'm telling you." I soften my tone with a wink. "Have a good day."

"But how will I find you?" It sounds like something out of a chick flick. It might even be a line from one of Christian's movies.

"It's a small town," I toss over my shoulder. "I'm sure you'll run into me."

I walk away, immediately forgetting about Prince Sebastian when my phone rings in my hand.

Finally, Safron is returning my call from L.A.

"It's difficult to do business with you when you don't return my calls," I inform her when I pick up.

"It's been busy here." There's no apology in her voice. "And some things came up. To be honest, Nina, I have some bad news."

I sit in my car and close my eyes, dreading her next words.

"What's up?"

"Well, Amanda and I have been talking," she begins, and I know, right here and now, that I'm about to be dumped. Over the phone. "I've had some personal things come up recently. I met a guy, and he's *amazing*, Nina. I just don't think I can relocate to Montana right now."

"And Amanda?"

"Cold feet," she says simply. "I'm sorry. Really. I wish it were different, but at least we're letting you know now before the business launches, and you're saddled with a bunch of clients and stuff."

"I can't believe this." I pinch the bridge of my nose. "We already had the attorney draw up the contracts. Paperwork was done. We filed the business name with the state. Basically, we've put out a lot of money for *nothing* to happen. Actually, let me rephrase. *I've* put out a lot of money."

"I'm sorry," she says again. Shortly after, she hangs up.

What the hell am I going to do now?

I don't mind eating alone. Actually, I don't mind doing most things alone. But going to a restaurant, getting a table, and eating by myself is actually something I enjoy.

I can people-watch. I get some thinking done. And I enjoy my own company.

Except tonight, because I've spent the entire day overthinking every aspect of my life.

I'm at the Snow Ghost Lodge restaurant at a table against the window, enjoying the sunset and the view. The lodge is on Whitetail Mountain, nestled in the ski resort village. Of course, it's September, so there's no skiing today, but the mountain boasts plenty of summer activities, as well. Hiking, downhill biking, zip-lining. You name it.

Thankfully, the summer rush of tourists is over. I've never seen anything like it, and I'm from southern California.

This little town of roughly seven-thousand ballooned up to almost a hundred thousand at any given time. It was insane.

I'm glad it's over.

I finish my meal and place my cloth napkin next to my plate just as my server comes over with a smile.

"Was everything okay?" Kyle asks. He's a young man, probably in his early twenties. He's handsome. Flirty. Way too young for me, but easy on the eyes.

"It was delicious, as always."

"Can I show you a dessert menu?"

I'm tempted. Sugar is my vice, but then I remember this morning at Drips & Sips and shake my head *no*.

"Just the check, please."

He sets the tab on the table, gathers my empty plate, and bustles away.

I take my time paying the bill, enjoying the last of the sunset as I finish my glass of wine.

Yes, eating alone in Cunningham Falls is lovely.

Once I've signed the receipt and gathered my handbag and light jacket, I walk toward the door.

"It's you."

I stop and glance down, surprised to see Sebastian smiling up at me.

"And it's you," I reply with a grin. "Are you okay? No visits to the ER?"

Sebastian laughs, and Jacob Baxter, the owner of the ski resort and a friend of Jenna's, watches us with interest.

"I take it you've met?" Jacob asks.

"Briefly," Sebastian replies, still watching me.

"I smacked right into him earlier," I add with

a shrug.

"She fell right into my arms. It must be fate."

I bust up laughing now, enjoying the banter. "Or Mercury is in retrograde, and I'm extra clumsy."

"Well, that's not romantic at all."

There's that word again.

Romantic.

"Sebastian, this is Nina Wolfe. She's a friend of my wife's."

"How is Grace?" I ask him. I like Jacob's wife very much. She's one of Jenna's best friends and has been nothing but kind to me.

"She's as beautiful as ever," Jacob replies with a smitten smile.

"Tell her I said hello."

"I'm happy to do that," he says.

"Are you here alone?" Sebastian asks.

Let me just say right now that listening to these men with their British accents is doing things to me. Sexy things.

It's just ridiculous.

"I am," I confirm.

"You're welcome to join us," Sebastian offers.

"Thank you, but I just finished eating. I'm headed home. Have a good evening, guys."

I nod and walk away, perfectly aware that Sebastian's gaze is pinned to my ass.

He's a hot one, that Sebastian. And he's even better-looking in person than in the magazines. Shouldn't that be illegal?

My house is situated along the lake, not far from the mountain turn-off. It only takes me about ten minutes to drive home. Once I'm inside, I strip out of my jeans and top and choose a pair of yoga shorts and a tank to be comfortable in.

When I'm on the couch, about to tackle the chore I've been avoiding all day—sending out emails to vendors that I already signed with, telling them that I have to either postpone or cancel altogether—my phone rings.

"Hi, Mom."

"Hello, dear," she says into my ear. Just from her tone, I can tell this is going to be a doozy of a conversation.

Pack your bags, we're going on a guilt trip.

"What are you up to, Mom?"

"Oh, you know, just watching some television. I'm quite sure I have cancer, by the way."

I roll my eyes, thankful that she didn't Face-Time me this time.

"Why do you say that?"

"I have painful urination."

Ew.

"It's probably just a UTI. You should go to the doctor."

"I don't have anyone to drive me."

"You have a car that Christian bought you. You can drive yourself."

"No, I couldn't possibly drive in my condition."

I take a long, deep breath. There's a reason Christian doesn't talk to our mother anymore. And I get it. I do. But it's left me in the middle and made me the one she calls to vent, or cry, or insist she's dying.

Because, according to her, she's dying every single day.

She's always needed a *lot* of attention, and not just from her children. She was an overbearing mom manager when Christian was young, and even stole a whole heap of his money. She was his power of attorney, and she took advantage of him. He's never forgiven her.

I don't blame him. But I wish I weren't the only one left to take care of her.

"You can always call a car service," I suggest.

"I don't know how to do that."

How are you a grown adult who can't take care of yourself? I want to scream it into the phone, but

I don't. Because that will only make things worse, and I don't want to hurt her feelings.

I may be a cold bitch, but even I'm not *that* cold.

"I will arrange it for you." I pull a notebook over to jot down a reminder. "What else have you been up to?"

"Just pining away for my children. I can't believe you moved so far away from me, Nina. You know how I rely on you. Christian is a grown man who can take care of himself."

"And you're a grown woman." The words are out of my mouth before I can stop them, and I cringe. "I'm sorry, Mom."

"No, it's what you mean." She's sniffling now. "I understand that your brother is your priority, and I'm just second-fiddle to him. It's fine."

For the love of all that's holy, make it stop.

"Mom, I love you both. I just needed a break from L.A. You know I'm not happy there."

"Well, then, maybe I should move up there. A mother should be with her children."

I feel my eyes go wide in panic.

No.

I don't want her here. And I know that makes me a horrible daughter, but I can't help it.

"I'll come visit soon."

"I see. You don't want me there either. Well, when I die of cancer, you'll be sorry. I already had a heart attack this year, it's only a matter of time."

She hangs up.

I drop my head back on the cushion of the couch and moan in defeat.

Because there is no winning with my mother. Ever.

My phone pings with a text. I don't want to look at it. I'm sure it's Mom, and anything she says right now will just irritate me more.

But guilt has me glancing down at the screen.

It's not my mom.

It's Fallon.

Fallon: Hey! That's all. Just hey.

I grin and reply.

Me: Hey yourself. What are you doing?

Fallon: Just sitting here by myself because Noah had to go rescue an owl. What are you doing?

Me: Trying not to feel guilty after telling my mom she's ridiculous.

Fallon: Your mom is ridiculous.

I laugh, feeling better.

Me: I know. But she still makes me feel guilty. It's her super-power.

Fallon: Take a deep breath. Will I see you at class in the morning?

Me: I think so. If not the morning, I'll come to the afternoon class.

Fallon: Sounds good. Lunch later in the week?

Me: Hell yes.

I love the water. I didn't know that I loved it as much as I do until I moved to Montana and bought my little house on the lake. But now that I have this home, I can't imagine ever living anywhere else.

I purchased a boat earlier this summer, and with the convenience of a boat slip in front of my house, I can come and go on the lake as I please.

It's the closest thing to Zen I've ever found, being on the lake. After no sleep, because I was too worried about the business and my mom and just *everything*, I decided I needed to take a boat ride early this morning.

It was the right call. I've only come across one other vessel, and we waved at each other as we sailed past. That's the other thing I love about being in a small town. Everyone's nice. I didn't think I'd enjoy that, but as it turns out, they're friendly, and while they do want to be in your business, they're not pushy about it.

It's the pushy that I hate.

This works for me.

I made some decisions this morning, about the things I struggled with all night long.

1. I'm dissolving the idea of the business. It makes me sad. I was excited to offer luxury services to the wealthy residents of Cunningham Falls. And trust me, there are plenty. Everything from housekeeping to culinary and party services. Pretty much anything a person could want, I could arrange it.

2. And two, I need to set some boundaries with my mother. I love her, but she can't manipulate me like this anymore. It's not fair.

I don't love the idea of giving up on the business, but I can't do it alone. I don't have the time, and I don't have staff. I needed Amanda and Safron.

And that's where I made my mistake. Depending on others only leads to blinding disappointment.

I sigh and steer the boat back to my slip, then frown when I see a tall figure standing at the end of my dock.

It's barely seven in the morning.

Suddenly, I'm convinced it's Brad Hull, Jenna's brother and the chief of police, here to tell me that my mom is dead. Or that something horrible happened to Christian.

But when I get closer, I see it's not Brad at all.

It's Sebastian.

I dock the boat, secure the ropes, and climb out, accepting Sebastian's proffered hand.

"Good morning," he says. Dark aviator sunglasses shield his blue eyes, and he's wearing khaki shorts and a polo shirt.

He looks like he's on his way to a photo shoot for a men's cologne advertisement.

"Hello," I say and push my hair out of my eyes. "Is the royal family aware they have a stalker on their hands?"

He laughs, his straight teeth white against his tanned skin.

"I'm not stalking you."

"Looks that way to me."

"You're the one who said it's a small town and I'd run into you. And I did, twice in one day."

"And now again, the very next day." I gesture for him to follow me up to the house. "How did you manage that, by the way?"

"After you left last night, I asked Jacob where you live."

I can't help but give him points for not lying. I like an honest man.

"Were you just going to crawl into bed with me?"

He stops walking, and I turn to face him, surprised to see the frown on his face.

"I'm not an arse," he says. "I was going to invite you to breakfast. I would have rung, but you refused to give me your number."

Okay, now *I* feel like the arse.

"I'm sorry. You're right. I'm just not a morning person, and I'm taking that out on you. I'm especially horrible when I haven't slept. Would you like some tea?"

"You have tea?"

"Of course, I do. I'm not an animal."

His lips twitch, and he walks forward. "Then I'd love some tea, Nina."

"Excellent. I can even whip together an omelet." Looks like I'll be missing the morning yoga class.

"A woman who can cook? Be still my heart."

CHAPTER 2

S HE'S RIGHT. IT'S insane that I'm here. I've never had to work this hard for a woman's number before.

It's bloody frustrating.

And intriguing, all at the same time.

Nina fills a kettle with water and fetches tins of tea from her cupboard, then turns to me with a small smile.

Jesus, she's beautiful. With her golden hair and bright blue eyes, she might be the loveliest woman I've ever seen.

And her sassy attitude just pulls at me.

"Earl Grey or peppermint?" she asks.

"Earl Grey would be wonderful, thank you."

She nods and builds our teas, and I fill the silence by looking at her cute home.

The house is small, but it has a wall of windows that face the lake. I imagine her sunset view is stunning. In the framed photos set out on shelves, I recognize Jacob's wife, Grace, along with Willa and Jenna. I've met them all in passing.

There's also a photo of Nina with Christian Wolfe—that's the connection that's kept niggling at the back of my mind—and Luke Williams, the movie star, with his wife.

"You're Christian Wolfe's sister," I say and turn to see her pouring hot water into mugs. Americans love their mugs. I'm accustomed to drinking my tea from a teacup, but I won't complain.

"Guilty," she replies and narrows her eyes as she plops teabags into the hot water.

"I knew I'd seen you before," I say, careful to keep my voice calm. I have a feeling this is a sticky conversation for her.

And why wouldn't it be? I'm sure many a person has tried to get close to Nina because of who her brother is.

I live that life every day.

But I couldn't care less who she's related to.

"I'm also his manager and publicist," she says with a shrug. "Though now that he's a boring, married man, things have calmed down quite a bit on that front."

"Less PR to worry about for a married man?" I ask her and take a seat in the chair she gestures to, the one across from her at the little, round table.

"It seems so. Fewer rumors, that's for sure. And he's doing less and less press these days."

"Which is probably easier for him, and less work for you."

Her eyebrows briefly pinch together, and I want to reach out and smooth my thumb over the lines there, but she quickly recovers and shrugs her shoulder once more.

"You could say that. Why don't you have security with you?"

Ah, a woman who cuts through the pleasantries and goes straight to the heart of the matter.

I like that very much.

"Because I told them not to come with me, much to everyone's dismay."

She adds a teaspoon of sugar to her cup and watches me as she stirs it. "I bet it pissed everyone off."

"More than you know," I agree. "But I don't need them here. I stick close to Jacob's resort, and few people know I'm here."

Nina's smart, I can see that. Her wheels are

turning like crazy. And she's used to the celebrity life—avoiding and dealing with scandal.

It seems my wheels are also turning.

"What do you think of Hollywood?" I ask.

"Why do you ask?"

"I'm curious."

"Well, it's not as glamorous as everyone thinks it is." She sips her tea thoughtfully. "It's a lot of smoke and mirrors. Window dressing, if you will. No one is the person they show to the media. Except Jennifer Garner. She might be the nicest person in the universe."

"I met her once," I agree with a nod. "She visited the palace about ten years ago when she was still married to Ben, and I have to agree. She's very kind."

Nina nods. "What do *you* think of being a celebrity?"

I press my lips together and rub my chin. I bloody hate being a celebrity.

But I was born into it.

I don't have a choice.

"It's a pain in the arse."

She laughs, making my blood sing through me. Her laugh is like a song, and the longer I sit here with her, the more attracted to her I become.

She's a siren.

"Don't sugarcoat it," she says.

"I rarely sugarcoat anything, much to my mother's dismay."

Nina watches me for a moment. "Me either."

"If you don't have to watch after your brother anymore, why are you in Montana? Why not go back to L.A.?"

"I hate L.A.," she mutters. "I hate the weather there, the people. *So* many people. The traffic. And my mom's there, and she's a handful."

"In what way?"

"She's needy. Dramatic. A hypochondriac. And she scammed my brother out of millions when he was young."

"Damn."

"Yeah. So, he doesn't speak to her anymore. I'm the one she calls to complain to."

"Your father?"

She shakes her head. "Gone when I was little. Mom left him because he was an alcoholic and moved us from Tennessee to L.A. I haven't seen him since."

"I'm sorry."

"I'm not. Who wants to hang out with an alcoholic?"

"Well, when you put it like that…"

Nina offers me more tea, and I accept. Wild horses couldn't drag me out of here now. I need to know more.

"Why are you in Montana?" she asks. "Besides to see Jacob."

"Seeing an old college mate isn't reason enough?"

She raises a brow. "You've spent a lot of time here."

"Should I be flattered that you pay such close attention?"

"I pay attention to everyone. It's my job. And having a prince in town is fodder for conversation, you know."

I nod slowly, trying to decide how much to tell her. "I needed a break. I was here over the winter and enjoyed it immensely. I trust Jacob to be discreet, affording me the luxury to be here without security."

"You feel safe here."

I blink at her. "Yes. I do."

She nods as if she understands perfectly. "I do, too. When Christian first came here, I felt sorry for him. He came to learn to ski for a movie role. I remember thinking, *poor Christian, he has to go rough it in the middle of nowhere.* Then I came to see him, almost ruined the best thing that's ever happened to him, but then helped to make it right and fell in love with Cunningham Falls in the process."

"You've been very busy."

She laughs, making me smile.

"You could say that."

"How did you almost ruin things for Christian?"

She frowns and sighs deeply. "I'm a bitch, Sebastian."

I stay quiet, waiting for her to continue. I don't doubt that she *can* be a bitch. I can sense that in her. But I also sense kindness and maybe even a little fear.

"I didn't think a small-town girl was good enough for *People* magazine's sexiest man alive," she says. "So, I came here and said some mean things to Jenna, which made her back right off. It crushed both of them."

She squirms in her seat.

"I still feel awful. I've apologized several times, and they both act like it's water under the bridge, but…" She trails off. I want to scoop her up and assure her that everything's okay.

I've never had that urge before.

"If they say they've forgiven you, you need to

believe them. Forgive yourself, Nina."

"Yeah." She blows out a breath. "Okay, back to you."

I cock a brow. I imagine this is where she'll ask me what it's like to be a prince.

"Do you prefer salty or sweet treats?"

I blink slowly, sure I've misheard her. "Excuse me?"

"Salty or sweet? This is important."

"Crisps are my favorite."

"Do you mean chips?"

I grin. "No, I mean crisps. Chips go with fish."

She smirks. "Ah, yes, your British lingo. So, you're a salty guy?"

"I suppose you could say that."

"Well, it was nice knowing you."

She stands and begins to clear the table.

"Are you blowing me off?"

"Absolutely. I'm a sweets girl. This is never going to work."

Now it's my turn to belly laugh. I can honestly say I've never been turned down because of my choice in junk food.

Nina is beautiful, funny, and intelligent.

Yes, I've found my girl.

She walks me to the door. When I stop to turn back to her, she's gazing up at me with humor-filled blue eyes.

"Have dinner with me tonight."

"I don't know, Sebastian. We're very different people."

"I'll eat all of the sugar in North America if you want me to."

She hooks a piece of hair behind her ear. "Well, there's that, but also the more obvious differences. You being of royal descent and all."

"It's just dinner."

She seems to think it over, then nods once. "Okay. Dinner it is."

"I'll pick you up at seven."

"Have you lost your fucking mind?"

Jacob's staring at me like I just told him I'm donating both kidneys.

I immediately drove back to the lodge from Nina's house and sought out my best friend to tell him my plan.

"Not the last time I checked, no."

"This is *never* going to work, mate. Your parents will kill you."

"Probably not kill. I guess they *could* have my disappearance arranged, but that hasn't happened in many years. They're much more civilized in their advanced ages."

"This isn't funny."

"It's also not the end of the fucking world," I remind him. "Jacob, your parents didn't choose a wife for you. You weren't in a fucking prison, just because of your birthright."

"I could understand going against their wishes if you found the love of your life and she was American. But that's not the case here. You don't love Nina."

"But *I'm* the one choosing her." I push my hands through my hair in frustration. "I will not marry someone my father chooses. You know him."

"Okay, so little thought to your happiness and *all* thought to what's best for the throne would go into the selection of the woman."

"Exactly. Not to mention, this law is archaic. It's ridiculous. This is not 1675, when the life expectancy of a man was forty if he was *lucky.* I'm not in danger of never having children and passing the throne down to other generations for God's sake."

"True. Not to mention, they did away with the tradition of marrying inside the bloodlines years ago."

We stare at each other for a moment, and then I shudder. "Thank Christ for that."

"But why couldn't you find a nice British woman? Sebastian, you'll have to give up the throne if you marry Nina. And that's *if* she agrees, which is a long shot. No offense, but Nina isn't exactly the type of woman who does what she's told."

"All the more reason that I like her. I don't want a woman who's been groomed to agree to everything I say. I want a challenge."

"Nina is challenging."

"She also understands what it means to be with a celebrity. She can handle scandals. She understands the press, the paparazzi. She knows what this life is like, better than anyone else. I never wanted the throne," I say quietly. "I told you that in university."

"I thought it would pass."

"It hasn't. Frederick has always been the one who should inherit the throne. He'll be an excellent king. He's already married to Catherine, who's amazing, and they have two children."

"But Fred's not the eldest son."

I shrug. "He should have been. Abdicating the throne is not something I take lightly. I understand the scandal. I understand it'll hurt my family. But, Jacob, *I don't want it.* If I could stop being royalty altogether, I would."

"No, you wouldn't."

I feel my lips twitch. "Okay, I wouldn't. But I do have a choice about the throne, and whom I choose to marry."

"When are you going to ask her?"

"I don't know. Soon. My birthday's coming up fast."

"Two months," Jacob reminds me. "Your mother's called me three times in the past week to ask when you're coming home because you won't call her back."

"I'll ring her."

Jacob shoves his hands into his pockets. "I can't talk you out of this?"

"No."

"Okay." He sighs deeply, but I already know what his next words will be. I can always depend on Jacob. "What do you need from me?"

I decide to wait a few days to ask her. I'll date her and get to know her better before I pop the question.

"You look absolutely amazing this evening."

It's true. She's sitting across from me at Ciao, the local Italian restaurant, reading her menu. Her sundress matches her blue eyes. Her hair is swept up in a pretty knot, and her makeup is tasteful and simple. She glances up at me with a flattered grin.

"Thank you."

"You're welcome."

The waitress arrives and stumbles through her speech of specials and wine recommendations.

"I'm sorry," she says with a sigh. "I don't usually serve a handsome prince."

"You're doing smashingly," I assure her. "I'm just a regular person, you know."

"Of course," she says with a shy nod.

I order us a bottle of nice French wine, and we place our food orders. Once the waitress is gone, I reach across the table for Nina's hand.

She seems surprised but doesn't pull away.

"How was the rest of your day?" Nina asks.

"Low-key. And yours?"

"Honestly?"

I nod.

"It sucked. But it's over, and this is my favorite restaurant, so it can only get better, right?"

"Why did you have a bad day?"

The waitress arrives with our wine before Nina can answer. I sniff and taste it, and upon my nod, our glasses are filled, and we're left alone again.

"This is delicious," Nina says.

"Don't avoid my question."

She smirks. "I tried. Well, it's kind of a long story."

"I conveniently have all evening. So, please, tell me the tale.."

"I was supposed to start a business here in Cunningham Falls next month with two of my friends from L.A. They were going to relocate here."

"What kind of business?"

"A luxury concierge service." She leans in. "Basically, whatever someone needed, we would provide. Do you need housekeeping services? We can find it. Need to throw your spoiled nine-year-old the birthday party of the century? Done. Car service? We can book that for you. You get the idea."

"It sounds great to me."

"Me, too. But, Safron and Amanda both pulled out yesterday, and I just don't have the means to do it alone."

"Is it the money?"

"Not at all. It's the physical and emotional resources. I need staff. I need *partners.* So, I dissolved the company, and spent the day reaching out to vendors that I already contracted with to tell them I wouldn't need their services after all."

"I'm sorry."

And I mean it. She looks defeated. I want to call those women and give them a piece of my mind.

"Me, too. But it's okay. I'll figure it out. It's just…with Christian not needing me like he once did, I need to fill my time with other things. I'm a workaholic, Sebastian. I enjoy working. But now I have to find something else."

I have just the thing for her. Being a princess is a full-time job, with obligations to charities and fundraisers and appearances to attend. She wouldn't be bored for a second.

But I can't mention that quite yet.

However, this entire conversation only reiterates for me that this arrangement will work perfectly for both of us.

Nina's phone pings, and she frowns as she checks it.

"I'm sorry," she says and sets her mobile aside. "Since my mom had a heart attack earlier this year, I keep my phone on me, just in case."

"That's understandable. Is everything okay?"

"Oh, that's her, but she's fine. Just needy."

"You mentioned that earlier. In what way is she needy?"

"She wants attention *all the time*. She calls every day, and that's fine. I don't mind talking to her, but she is the queen of the guilt trip. If every conversation didn't end with her sighing unhappily and hanging up on me, our daily chats would be much more pleasant."

"I admit, my mother can be overbearing, as well. I think that's a mother's job. But even when I make decisions she doesn't agree with, she never hits me with the guilt trip."

"You're lucky. Your mother is gorgeous, by the way."

"Inside and out." That reminds me, I need to call her. "And she's an excellent queen."

"Does she walk around the palace in a tiara?" Nina asks. "I've always wondered that."

"No." I laugh and sit back as our meals are delivered. "She's usually casual in a simple dress."

"No slacks or jeans?"

I frown and reach for pepper. "No. Royal women aren't permitted to wear slacks, and certainly not jeans."

"Wow. Even in the twenty-first century?"

"My sister-in-law did wear maternity pants when she was pregnant because it was more comfortable for her, and she had a tough pregnancy. But aside from that, no."

Nina chews on her lasagna thoughtfully. "I think I would hate that."

"You're wearing a dress now."

"I know, but I'd want to *choose* what I wore. I wouldn't like to be given a dress code. I mean, I understand for formal or state events, that sort of thing. But day-to-day? They'd kick me out for wearing jeans."

"I admit, it is an archaic rule. But aside from the dresses, women have as many rights as men in my country."

"That's good."

The rest of our dinner is full of interesting conversation and fun banter. At one point, Nina reaches across the table with her napkin to wipe red sauce from the corner of my lips.

I can't remember when or if I've ever enjoyed myself more.

When it's finally time to take her home, I walk her to her door and wait while she unlocks it. When she turns to me, I drag my thumb down her cheek and watch the way her eyes light up in the moonlight.

"You're absolutely lovely, Nina."

I lean in and gently brush my lips over hers. That one touch isn't enough, and I sink into her, pinning her against the doorjamb. She moans and shoves her hands into the hair at the nape of my neck, holding on tightly as we ride the wave of lust and attraction.

Her body is tight and firm. Strong. And fits against me as if she were bloody made for me.

I can't get enough of her.

When we pull away to catch our breath, I cup her face in my hands and look deeply into her eyes.

"You need to marry me."

CHAPTER 3

I CLEARLY HAD too much wine. Or, maybe I've been hit on the head, and I'm unconscious, and this whole thing is a dream.

Because I *know* I'm not just finishing up a date with the freaking Prince of England where he just proposed marriage.

Wait, that's not right. He didn't ask.

He told.

"Say something," he says quietly, watching me intently.

"I'm sure I misheard you."

He sighs and gestures toward my house. "Let's go inside, and we can talk."

I lead the way, turning on lights and walking

through my space to the living room. I sit on the couch, cross my legs, and watch as Sebastian paces the room, rubbing his hand over his lips in agitation.

I'm fascinated.

"You need to marry me, Nina."

"What was in that wine she gave us?"

He smiles and sits across from me, his elbows braced on his knees as he watches me with those bright blue eyes. "I'm being serious."

"Sebastian, I know I'm a pretty great catch, but even I can't make someone fall in love with me in the span of roughly thirty-six hours."

He licks his lips. "You're right. I'm not suggesting we marry because I'm in love with you."

"I'm flattered."

"And I don't mean to offend you by saying that. We're both adults here."

I nod and wait for him to continue. Although, I should stop him. I'm *never* getting married, remember?

"In addition to coming here to see Jacob, I've also been on the lookout for a bride. You see, I'm coming up on my thirty-fifth birthday."

I narrow my eyes, listening.

"In my country, the law states that if the heir to the throne is not married by the time he reaches thirty-five, a suitable wife will be chosen by the king."

"Wow, that's archaic."

His lips twitch. "My thoughts exactly."

"So, you're looking for a suitable wife so *you're* the one who chooses, rather than your father?"

"You're perceptive as well as intelligent," he says.

"But I'm not British. And even I know that, in order for you to be king, you have to marry a British woman."

He nods slowly. "I will abdicate my claim to the throne after we wed. I won't be king."

I sit back in surprise, watching as Sebastian swallows hard, then looks down at his hands before looking back up at me.

"Why me?"

"Isn't that obvious?"

"No. No, it's not. I need you to enlighten me because I'm definitely not what I would consider princess material."

"Aside from the fact that you're beautiful, I enjoy spending time with you. You're also highly intelligent, and you know how to work with celebrities, and what it means to be in a world where you're constantly under scrutiny. You'll be able to handle the pressures that come with being in my family. And let me tell you, there are plenty of them."

"So, you're saying you want to marry me because of my resume?"

He blinks once. "That sounds way worse than I intended. Please know that I think very highly of you, Nina. I wouldn't suggest this if I didn't."

I take a long, deep breath. It's true, I don't plan to ever marry. Certainly not for love. Love is fleeting. Fickle. It comes and goes with the phase of the moon or a woman's hormonal cycle.

It's not forever.

But this? This is different.

"You're awfully quiet," Sebastian says at last, watching as I chew my lip.

"I'm thinking," I murmur.

I can't believe I'm even entertaining this. It's insane!

But at the same time, it sounds like an adventure. A challenge. Have I not been searching for exactly that?

"If you're looking for compensation, I'm sure we can work something out."

Okay, that pisses me off.

"I'm not a whore."

My tone is calm, my voice cool.

"That's not what I was implying."

"Well, offering to pay me for my services is doing exactly that. I don't need your money. I have plenty of my own."

I stand now and walk to the windows. The night sky is so dark, I can't see the shoreline tonight.

"I'm sorry. But you have to get something out of this."

He moves behind me. He doesn't touch me, but I can hear the regret in his voice.

"Adventure," I whisper. "Change. A sense of purpose."

I turn and stare up at him. Into those bright eyes.

"I'll marry you," I say at last and hold my hand up before he can speak. "I'll pretend to be in love with you, if that's what you need."

"I do."

"If this evolves into something intimate, I'm okay with that. I feel the chemistry between us."

"Thank God, because I've had a hell of a time keeping my hands to myself."

I smile now, enjoying him.

"But, Sebastian, I'll never fall in love with you. You need to know that now."

His eyes narrow, and he's quiet for a long moment, watching me in silence.

"Loving me isn't a requirement," he says at last.

For some reason, that bothers me. *I'm* the one who just said no to love, yet for reasons I can't grasp, hearing him say that he doesn't have to be loved hits me wrong.

"Then it seems we have a deal."

He reaches for my hand and lifts it to his lips. He presses a kiss to my finger, where a ring will eventually go.

"We'll choose this together," he says and then kisses my wrist, then the inside of my elbow. Finally, he pulls me to him and covers my mouth with his.

Prince Sebastian is a hell of a kisser.

I didn't sleep last night.

I mean, I guess it's not unusual to lose sleep after a handsome prince proposes. Especially when it's laid out as a business deal.

All night, I bounced between excitement and feeling as if I'd lost my ever-loving mind.

I agreed to marry a freaking *prince*.

I barely know him.

I don't love him.

At least I'm attracted to him. If he hadn't backed away last night and promised to see me today, I would have stripped naked and begged him to fuck me, right then and there, romance novel-style.

Thank God I didn't do that. I at least have a little dignity left.

I spent the rest of my night on the computer, pouring over articles on the royal family, learning names and protocols. It occurred to me around two in the morning that I'd have to *meet* the King and Queen of England. How should I address them? What's the etiquette?

I had no idea.

So, I read articles and even a short book on how to behave around royals.

It was fascinating.

When it comes time to meet them, I hope I don't forget everything I just read and behave like a complete idiot.

Now, I'm sitting on the deck, eating a grilled cheese sandwich with Doritos—not the breakfast of champions, I know, but don't judge me. I've had an overwhelming two days—when I hear a car pull in.

"I'm back here!" I call out when I hear the door slam shut. Sebastian walks around and up the steps to the deck, smiling. "Good morning."

"And the same to you."

I stand and lower myself into a deep curtsy.

"Your Royal Highness."

I stand to find Sebastian staring at me, blinking slowly. "Where did you learn that?"

"Google." I sit back in the chair and pop a Dorito into my mouth. "I was up all night studying."

"Studying what?"

"Royal etiquette."

He sits across from me and snags a handful of chips. "These are my favorite."

"Mine, too."

"You didn't have to study all of that stuff. You could have just asked me."

"No. I had stupid questions. Better to use Google."

"Well, I hate to tell you this, and I love that you put in the work, but that curtsy was all wrong."

I stare at him and then frown. "I practiced for an hour."

"You would have been better off sleeping." He brushes the cheese powder from his fingers and stands. "It's really very simple."

His voice is high now, as if he's a woman, and it makes me giggle.

"You don't have to bend yourself in half like they do in the Disney movies. It's a simple little motion like this."

He pops one foot behind the other, and barely moves his body as he lowers his head.

"That looks way easier." I stand with him and mimic his movements.

"Perfect. You've mastered it." We retake our seats and dig into the chips. "The rest of it? You'll learn as we go. It takes years to learn everything. We're taught from the time we're in nappies how to behave. You can't expect to know everything within a few hours."

"I'm totally intimidated," I admit. Before I know what's happening, Sebastian pulls me out of my seat and into his lap.

"You'll be brilliant. You have manners, you know how to behave in public. That's really all you need to know to start."

"Somehow, I think you're dumbing it all down for me."

His grin flashes before he kisses me soundly and puts me back on my feet.

"We have an appointment, darling."

"Where?"

"Cunningham Falls Goldsmiths," he says. "You need a ring on your gorgeous finger. If I'd truly been thinking before I left London, I would have grabbed one from the vault, but it didn't occur to me. We can choose something different at the palace later, but I want to put something on your finger right away."

"I don't need anything from the palace."

"Oh, trust me. There will be all kinds of speculation about your ring. Who made it, whose stones are in it. It's a thing."

"Whose stones are in your mom's ring?"

"Queen Victoria's," he says absently as he rolls the top on the bag of chips and helps me clear the table, carrying everything inside. "People love tradition, and wearing old jewels is one the people love to see on their royals."

"This is a lot."

He stops and looks at me, all humor gone from his face. "We're just starting, Nina. If you can't or won't do this, I need to know now."

"I can and will," I reply immediately. "There's just so much more to consider than I realized."

"You'll be amazing," he assures me and takes my hand, leading me to his rental car. He drives me the short distance to downtown and parks in front of a tiny jewelry shop.

We step inside and are greeted warmly by a couple, both who appear in their early fifties.

"Hi, I'm Kate." The pretty, tall blonde holds out her hand for mine. "And this is my husband, Aric. We own this shop and are happy to help with anything you need."

"We need an engagement ring," Sebastian says with a smile.

"Oh, that's lovely. Congratulations." Kate smiles at her husband. "Aric is the goldsmith. I do design work. So, if you don't see something here in the cabinet, we can make something custom."

"What's your budget?" Aric asks as he and Kate begin pulling black velvet trays from the back.

"There is no budget," Sebastian replies.

My gaze whips up to his. "No, that's cra—"

"No budget," he repeats with a wink. "My darling can have whatever she wants."

He kisses my hand, and a piece of me melts. Goodness, this man is potent.

We spend the next hour looking over rings, discussing stone shape and size, metal type, and everything else imaginable. My brain is mushy as I stare down at a five-karat cushion-cut diamond set in platinum.

It costs more than my house.

"I can't believe you have this in this little shop in Montana."

"The shop is deceiving," Aric says with a grin.

"We can satisfy any budget or taste."

"Are you sure?" I ask Sebastian.

He simply passes a black American Express card to Kate and smiles down at me. "It suits you."

"This would suit anyone," I murmur.

Once we're back in the car, we sit and stare at each other for a moment, then smiles break out on both of our faces.

"It's official," I say and hold up the ring. "You put a ring on it."

"I'm going to take a photo and post it…somewhere. I don't have social media, as it's frowned upon, but—"

"No." I shake my head adamantly. "That is *not* how you do this. We'll go to my brother's house and let *him* post the picture."

"This is why you're perfect," Sebastian says as he starts the car. "Just tell me where to go."

I call ahead so I don't catch Christian and Jenna by surprise, and when we pull into the driveway, Jenna's standing in the doorway, waiting.

"What is going on?" she asks as we step inside. "Hello, Sebastian."

"Hello, Jenna." He kisses both of her cheeks, and when Christian walks into the room, Sebastian shakes my brother's hand. "Christian."

Christian looks at me, then Sebastian, and back

to me again.

"Holy shit," Jenna says, reaching for my hand. "Look at this rock!"

"What in the hell is going on?" Christian demands.

"We need to sit down," I say, blowing out a breath. "I'm going to explain everything."

Sebastian frowns down at me, and when the others turn their backs to walk to the dining room, I whisper up to him, "They're all I have. They're safe."

He nods, and we follow the couple, sitting across from them at the table.

"We're getting married," I say softly.

"You literally said three days ago that you'd *never* get married," Jenna reminds me, and I feel Sebastian stare down at me.

"Is that true?"

"Oh, yeah." I shrug a shoulder. "But we're not getting married because we're in love."

Christian's squinted eyes narrow even further. I'm shocked that he can even see through them.

Sebastian briefly outlines what he said to me last night. When he comes to a close, Christian is shaking his head back and forth.

He's going to give himself whiplash.

"No," my brother says. "Absolutely not."

"Why?" I demand. "Because I'm not tripping over myself with love and hearts? That's ridiculous."

"No," Christian counters. "Because you met him ten minutes ago, Nina. You don't know him."

I take a deep breath.

"Not to mention," he continues, "you *don't* love him. And he hasn't said a word about keeping you safe and taking care of you."

"She's perfectly safe with me, always," Sebastian says. His voice is hard.

"I'm an adult, Christian. I know you're protective, and you're looking out for me. I know what that feels like." I glance at Jenna and smile. "But at the end of the day, I'm a grown woman who can make her own choices. I'm here, telling you out of courtesy, not obligation."

"She's right," Jenna says, holding onto her husband's hand. "Your sister doesn't make rash decisions."

"Exactly." I smile at my sister-in-law.

"I don't like it," Christian says. "I'm saying that right now. I'm not saying you're a bad man. I like you. But this is sudden, and she's my *sister.*"

"I understand," Sebastian says. "I honestly do."

Christian sighs. "What do you need from me?"

"I need you to take a photo of us and post it on your Instagram."

"You're smart," Jenna says with a slow grin. "It'll go viral within ten minutes."

"Are you sure?" Christian leans onto the table, watching me intently. "Once I post this, there's no turning back. It'll be a social media shitstorm within minutes. You *know* this."

"I know."

With his eyes still pinned to mine, he pulls his phone out of his pocket.

"You should cuddle up," Jenna instructs. "And, Nina, put your left hand on his cheek so we can see that killer ring. Holy crap, it's beautiful."

Sebastian's skin is warm and smooth against mine. He presses his lips to my forehead, and I close my eyes.

"That's the one," Jenna breathes. "Make it black and white, and it's perfect."

Christian fiddles with his phone and turns it so we can see the photo.

It's black and white. Sebastian is kissing my forehead. My eyes are closed, and a smile is just tickling my lips.

The ring is front and center.

It looks like a sweet, intimate moment that was captured unexpectedly.

"Do it," Sebastian says.

"Won't the palace be pissed that they didn't approve this?" I ask him.

"The palace is going to be pissed about a lot of things."

"I'd better call my mother," Sebastian says as he drives me home. "I don't want her to hear about this from the social media director on staff."

"You have that?"

"Of course." He pulls into the driveway and follows me inside. "I'll step out onto the deck. I won't be long."

"I'll brew you some tea."

He stops and turns to me, surprise on his handsome face. "You don't have to do that."

"I think you'll need it after this call."

He kisses me on the forehead again and steps outside.

I can't hear what he's saying, but I can see his body language. His whole frame is tight as he stands facing the water, one hand in his pocket, the other holding the phone to his ear as he waits for someone to pick up. After a few moments, he starts to pace as he speaks. He pushes his hand through his hair in agitation.

It's clearly not going well.

The kettle whistle blows, catching my attention. I'm pouring our tea when my own phone rings.

It's my mother.

"Hello."

"What in the ever-loving hell are you doing, Nina?"

I close my eyes, grateful that Sebastian is still outside.

"Why do you ask?"

"Don't you play stupid with me, young lady. I saw the news. What do you have to say for yourself?"

CHAPTER 4

Nina

THIS IS IT. This is my opportunity to draw a line in the sand and tell my mom to back off. To mind her own business.

I need to set boundaries.

And with any other person in my life, doing that comes easily.

With my mom? Different story.

"Nina."

"You obviously already know what's going on," I say at last and lean my hip on the countertop edge, facing away from Sebastian. "The news has it pretty much right."

"You're marrying *Prince Sebastian*?"

"Yes." I bite my lip. "I'm in love with him, and

he asked me to marry him. I said yes."

"You didn't even tell me you were dating anyone, not to mention a freaking prince!"

"We were keeping it on the down-low."

"I can't believe you let me hear about it this way. I am your *mother*, Nina Marie. You should tell me these things." She starts to sniffle, and I roll my eyes. I want nothing more than to hang up the phone.

Is it ironic that both Sebastian and I are breaking the news to our mothers at the same time?

"I don't understand why you've pulled away from me so completely. You're my *only daughter.* It's bad enough that my son, the boy I worked so hard for, to make him who he is today, has blown me off. But now you, as well? How could you, Nina?"

"Mom, stop." My voice is hard, surprising both of us. "Stop it with this guilt trip. I'm sick and tired of listening to you whine about how wrong we've done you. You're sitting in a million-dollar house in Manhattan Beach, with a killer view, and everything else you could ever need. You *stole* from Christian and made his life a living hell for years. Yet he still makes sure you're financially secure. And you smother me."

I cover my mouth with my whole hand, shocked that I just spewed all of that at my mother. Words

I've wanted to say for *years*.

Part of me feels ashamed for being disrespectful. The other part gives myself a high-five.

"How dare you?"

"I'm done, Mom. I love you, but I won't be treated like this anymore. You're welcome to call me when you can treat me with respect."

And with that, I end the call and hang my head in my hands, shaking from the adrenaline of it all.

"I'm proud of you."

I whirl at the sound of Sebastian's voice and cringe in embarrassment. "I wish you hadn't heard that."

"I'm glad I did." He walks to me and takes my hand. "Are you all right?"

"I will be. It was a long time coming, but it doesn't make me feel any less guilty. How did your call go?"

"A bit better than yours, but my mum isn't delighted with me either."

"So, we're both disappointments then."

He smiles and tugs me in for a hug. I've never been one for physical affection. But this is nice.

"You always stiffen up when I pull you into my arms, but then you relax."

"I don't like to be touched," I say into his chest,

listening to his heartbeat.

"Well, we'll need to work on that, darling, because I'm an affectionate fellow, and you're about to be my wife."

"But we're not falling in love."

"That doesn't mean I can't care for you, Nina. Enjoy you. Touch you. You said yourself the other night, you feel the chemistry."

I sigh and grip him just a bit tighter. "I did say that. And I do feel it."

"Then why fight it?"

"I'm not. I'm just adjusting. I think there will be plenty to adjust to."

"For both of us," he agrees and loosens his hold on me. "I also spoke with Charles, my security detail chief. He's on his way here. They should arrive late tonight. He's quite livid."

"Nothing is happening."

His eyes take on a hint of sadness as he drags his knuckles down my cheek.

"Yet," he says. "We'll be mobbed by paparazzi by morning."

"Jesus." I drag my hand down my face and pace away from him, my mind whirling.

"It seems our brief time in our little bubble here in Montana is almost over," he continues. "Do you mind if I go up to the resort and fetch my things?

It's probably simpler if we can base out of here."

"Of course, I don't mind. But maybe you shouldn't go. We can call up and ask Jacob to get your stuff and bring it here."

He smiles gently. "Are you worried for me, darling?"

"Maybe a little."

"I'll be fine. And I won't be long. Lock up tight. No sitting out on the deck this evening, at least not until my security arrives."

"I can call Brad. Jenna's oldest brother is the police chief in Cunningham Falls."

"That's a great idea," he says with a nod. "Let's do that, and I'll go get my things."

But he doesn't turn away. He leans in and kisses me, softly at first, but then he really sinks in and kisses me. Like his damn life depends on it.

Is this what they mean when they talk about being kissed silly? It's new for me.

I don't hate it.

"I'll be back soon," he murmurs against my lips, and then he's gone. Once he pulls out of my driveway, I stand with my fingertips pressed against my lips and take a deep breath.

Seems someone can give me butterflies, after all.

"I have ten men on the house," Brad says two hours later. His face is grim. "I just got off the phone with Charles, and we agree that you both need to stay put inside the house."

"There is literally no reason for that," I say, trying to sound reasonable. "Brad, it's only been *hours* since the news went out on social media. There's no way the paparazzi has already made it to town to make our lives hell."

"You underestimate them," Sebastian says beside me. His arms are crossed over his chest. "We'll stay here."

"I have the driveway blocked off. No one in a vehicle can get in or out without speaking with my guys. I also have a helicopter on standby to give us air support."

I scowl. "This feels…excessive."

"It's not enough." A tall man with salt and pepper hair marches into the house, his face grim. He stops before Sebastian and bows his head. "Your Royal Highness."

"Hello, Charles."

"I'd like a word with you please, sir."

"You can speak with me right here, Charles."

The man, whose face is nothing if not moody

as hell, looks around at all of us in the room and then back to Sebastian.

"How did you get here so fast?" I blurt.

Charles' cold gaze meets mine. "I can get to His Royal Highness no matter where he is in the world within hours. Our military planes are quite advanced, miss."

"Wow."

"Charles, this is Nina," Sebastian says.

"I recognize her."

Sebastian raises an eyebrow, and Charles immediately turns to me, bowing his head. "It's a pleasure to meet you, miss."

"The pleasure is mine, Charles."

I try to carry on like normal, but three words keep ringing in my ears.

Your Royal Highness.

I'm marrying a prince. What in the actual hell do I think I'm doing?

Charles turns back to Sebastian. "I would hope, after nearly twenty years of working with you, that you would have thought to call me before this whole storm began so I could be on hand and at the ready to protect you, sir."

"You're here now, Charles. And I appreciate it."

I can see Sebastian's body is tense again. Is it because he doesn't like to be told what to do by his staff? Or is he really worried about not being safe here in Cunningham Falls?

Without looking my way, he reaches over and links his hand with mine. The touch immediately calms me. And if I'm not mistaken, Sebastian's body relaxes a bit, as well.

"We'll leave first thing in the morning," Charles says and looks at Sebastian. "I have orders to bring you home right away."

"I'll agree because I've spoken with my mother and there's plenty to do back in London. But, Charles, you need to watch yourself with me. Twenty years of service is admirable, but you're not my father."

"Sir." He bows his head. Without another word, he bustles out of the room.

"He's an intense one, isn't he?" Brad asks. "I'll go confer with him. He'll have access to as many of my men as he needs. Before I leave, I wanted to say congratulations."

"Thanks, Brad."

"My pleasure." He nods and then exits the room. The rest of the people go with him, leaving Sebastian and me alone.

It's late. It's been a *long* day.

"Let's go to the bedroom," I suggest. "It's more private."

He doesn't reply, just stands and walks with me, up the stairs to my bedroom. When we're closed up inside, I let out a long sigh and sit on the end of the bed.

"I don't know if I've ever been this tired."

"Are you okay?"

"I'm fine. It's just a lot of information." I look up at him. "Aren't you scared? Of what your parents will say? Of what the *people* will say?"

"A little," he admits. "I wouldn't be human if I weren't. But what I'm about to go through isn't nearly as challenging as what I'm about to ask of you. And I have to say, right here and now, thank you, Nina."

"You make it sound like I'm going to the guillotine."

"There might be moments when it feels like it," he concedes. "But I assure you, I'll be right with you, every step of the way. You're not alone in this. I appreciate you so much, and I *will* protect and care for you. I hope you believe that."

"I do." I smile at him. "I do believe that. You have my back. And I have yours."

The next morning, I find myself packing my suitcases, getting ready to go to England. How long will we be there? I have no idea, so I basically have to take everything.

Except, nothing I have is appropriate.

"Why are you scowling like that?" Sebastian asks as he walks into my bedroom to find me glaring at my suitcase.

"I don't have princess clothes." I turn to him, panic beginning to set in. "Sebastian, I literally only have like *five* things that are appropriate, and even those aren't designer. I've never had a need for it. And now I'm about to meet the freaking *King and Queen of England*!"

"Actually, they reign over the commonwealth countries. Not just England."

I take a deep breath, but it doesn't help the anxiety that's just grabbed hold of my neck.

"Holy shit."

"Hey, you're going to be smashing," he says. "Show me your curtsy again."

I roll my eyes. "No. I'm horrible at it."

"Well, then you need to practice. Show me."

"You go first."

His lips twitch. "Now listen carefully."

His voice is high-pitched again, and it makes me laugh. I love his silly side.

"It's easy, really. All you do is this."

He executes a perfect curtsy and then gestures for me to follow. Which I do, and am relieved that it's not so bad.

"Excellent."

"And what do I call them?"

"Your Majesty, when you first meet them. After that, it's sir or ma'am."

"Well, that's easy, at least."

Sebastian tugs me to him and lightly kisses my lips. His hand glides down my spine to my ass, and then up again.

"You could distract me by getting me naked," I suggest and watch as his eyes darken with lust.

We were too tired last night. We just fell onto the bed and slept. This morning, we've been busy getting ready to leave for London.

"The first time I strip you bare and have you writhing beneath me will not be when there are twenty men downstairs waiting for us. It'll be when I can take my time with you, explore every inch, every curve. I want to make you gasp and moan and lose your bloody mind."

"This is a good start." My voice is breathy to my own ears. But his chin is firm, and I know he won't back down.

Which is for the best because he's right, there

are too many people in my house.

"Okay. I still don't know what to pack."

"Don't worry about it," he replies. "It'll be taken care of for you."

"What does that mean?"

"Exactly what it sounds like. You're about to marry into the royal family, Nina. That means you'll have every need taken care of, every whim provided for. Just pack what you might miss, and we'll worry about the rest later."

I don't have time to ask questions. So I throw some clothes, the toiletries I can't live without, and my blow-dryer into the suitcase, and I'm ready to go.

I move to carry my bag, but Sebastian shakes his head.

"Someone will get that for you."

"I'm perfectly capable—"

"It's their job, Nina. Honest. They're being paid well to carry your bags."

I shrug. "If you say so."

Once we're downstairs, we're quickly bustled into the waiting car. As we drive down my driveway, my eyes feel as if they're going to bug out of my face.

"There must be hundreds of them."

Sebastian takes my hand. I'm grateful that the glass is tinted, and the cameras can't take photos of us as we crawl past. The driver is careful not to hit anyone.

"They all appeared overnight."

"They came around two in the morning," Sebastian says.

"How do you know? You were with me."

"Charles briefed me this morning," he says.

"I need to let Christian know."

I pull out my phone, but Sebastian shakes his head.

"I already spoke with him, as well. He knows what's going on, and Brad has extra security watching their house. I'm so sorry this happened, Nina."

"It's not your fault." I sit back, relieved when the car is able to pick up the pace, driving faster to the airport.

"Charles is leaving four men behind to watch your house," Sebastian says. "They'll be staying there. I'm sorry, it can't be avoided. You just don't have enough security to leave it unoccupied."

"I figured that would happen. I'll work on building a better security plan later."

"No need, miss," Charles says from the front seat. "We will take care of it for you."

I glance at Sebastian in surprise. He just smiles.

"Thank you."

CHAPTER 5

Sebastian

"THAT WAS THE fastest flight of my life," Nina murmurs beside me and then takes a deep breath.

"It was actually a short flight, compared to commercial flights to Europe," I reply and smile when she looks up at me. Her eyes are a bit glassy—from exhaustion or fear, I'm not sure which.

Possibly both.

"No one even asked for my passport."

"No, darling." I kiss her fingers and rest our hands on my thigh. Charles is sitting up with the driver, and it's important that we look like a couple in love.

Not to mention, I quite enjoy touching her.

"I've read all of the articles," she mutters as if to herself. "It's going to be fine."

It's going to be fine.

Eventually.

But these first few days will be rough. I wish I could protect her from the scrutiny of my family's gaze. The staff. The public.

They won't like that Nina's American. And they certainly won't like that I'm marrying her. If it were my youngest brother, Callum, it wouldn't matter as much. He's third in line for the throne, so he can marry pretty much anyone he chooses.

As for the heir? Well, there are different rules.

And I'm about to upset the entire applecart.

"Have you been to London before?" I ask Nina, hoping to get her to relax a bit.

"Sure," she says. "I've been several times with Christian, mostly for movie premieres. I haven't had a chance to really explore much, though. It's a beautiful city."

"I'll show it to you," I reply. "I can get some behind-the-scenes tours."

"I should hope so," she says with a laugh. "What's the point in reigning over everything the eye can see if there aren't some perks?"

She's about to discover that I have more *perks* than just being able to roam around the Tower of

London whenever I please.

We arrive at the palace, and the gates open to allow the cars through. There is a vehicle ahead of us and behind us, both full of security.

Tourists line the thirty-foot-tall fence, taking photos and hoping to get a glimpse of a member of the royal family.

The king's flag flies on top of the palace, signaling that he's in residence. If he's gone, either traveling or at one of the other palaces, the country's flag flies instead.

"We'll go to my flat to freshen up," I inform Charles, who nods silently. Charles has always been a stern man, but he seems especially angry with me now. I know he feels like I'm putting myself at risk. He doesn't just take his job seriously, he cares about my entire family and me.

When the car stops behind a rock wall, keeping us hidden from prying eyes, I lead Nina into the palace and down the long hallway to my home.

"There are five flats in the palace," I inform her. "One for me and each of my siblings and another for my parents. Then there are public areas, open to tours when we're not in residence. We also host parties here, entertain heads of state, that sort of thing."

"It's enormous," she says, her eyes roaming over paintings of ancestors long dead, tapestries, and rugs.

Each piece has a story, of course.

"We're in here." I open the door to my quarters and glance back at Charles. "We're fine. I'll meet with you later."

"Sir." He bows his head and then marches off, speaking into a device as he goes.

"This is your apartment?"

"It is."

I watch as she steps out of her heels, wiggling her toes against the eight-hundred-year-old rug in my living room.

She bites her lip and stares at me, and I can see that the reality of our arrangement has finally truly hit home for her.

"Come here." I walk to her and pull her into my arms, rocking us both back and forth. "I'll make sure you're more than comfortable here."

"It's a castle."

"No, I'll show you a castle another day."

She chuckles against my chest.

Before I can say anything else, there's a knock at the door, and my assistant, Harrison, walks in. He's younger than I am but has the straight posture and stick-up-his-ass pose mastered.

"Your Royal Highness," he says, bowing his

head. "It's a pleasure to have you home, sir."

"Thank you, Harrison. I'd like to introduce you to Nina. My fiancée."

His head snaps up in surprise. It seems Harrison hasn't heard the scuttle yet, but then again, that's one of the reasons I like having him on my staff. He doesn't give a shit about rumors.

"Sir?"

"That's right. Nina Wolfe, this is my personal assistant, Harrison."

"Hello," Nina says politely. "It's nice to meet you."

"You as well, miss."

"Where's my boy?"

Mary, my sister's former lady-in-waiting, rushes through the doorway. She's in her late seventies, round as can be, and one of my favorite people of all time.

"Hello, Mary."

"I'm so relieved you're home," she says. She's never been one to bow or use titles. She's a motherly type that all of my siblings and I love.

"This is Nina. Nina, this is Mary. She's retired now, but she was my sister Eleanor's lady-in-waiting. I asked her to come and help you while we're here. She knows everything there is to know about my family, and I believe she'll be a great asset to you."

"And a friend," Mary adds, taking Nina's hand in hers. "Oh, love, you look just knackered. I wish I had time to put you to bed for a while, but I'm afraid we haven't time for it. We need to freshen you up."

"Your parents are expecting you in about thirty minutes," Harrison adds.

Nina watches me with wide eyes, so I nod reassuringly. "You're in excellent hands with Mary. I'll be here, waiting for you."

"Come on, dear." Mary herds Nina out of the room, and I'm left alone with Harrison.

"I should change, as well." I walk to my bedroom with Harrison on my heels. The staff has already prepared a bedroom with a dressing space for Nina. Along with a whole closet full of clothes and shoes.

Our staff works fast.

"How did I miss that she's your fiancée?" Harrison asks. Now that we're alone, he's much more casual. Harrison is not only my PA, he's also one of my best mates.

"It's rather recent," I reply, choosing fresh clothes to change into. "And I'm sorry I didn't call you. It's been a busy twenty-four hours."

"Your parents are likely going to murder you.

They'll reintroduce beheadings."

"I've never known you to be so dramatic."

But he's not laughing. "I'm not kidding, Sebastian. This has disaster written all over it."

"Such is my life, mate." I tie my necktie and throw on the light gray jacket that matches my slacks. "This first meeting will be the most uncomfortable."

"She's walking into the lion's den."

"I'll be with her."

I sigh and prop my hands on my hips, desperately trying to keep my nerves at bay. "Just be my friend here, okay?"

"She's beautiful," he says. "And if she makes you happy, then I'm happy. I hope I still get to work for you after they fire you from the next in line position."

"I'll see to it." I nod and walk into the sitting room just as Nina does the same. My steps falter, as if my feet are suddenly rooted to the floor.

My God, she's gorgeous in a simple pink dress with cap sleeves and black heels.

"You're stunning," I say at last. "If my parents don't see that, they're no relatives of mine."

She smiles softly. "Thank you. You look nice, as well." She dips into her curtsy, perfectly this time. "Your Royal Highness."

"Good girl," Mary says with a wink. "We've practiced that one."

"You're simply lovely," I say and offer Nina my arm, which she takes. My hand covers her small one as we walk to the door. "What do you think of Mary?" I ask after we've left my flat and are alone.

"She's amazing. I want to keep her. She's already given me so much advice. I'm going to learn so much from her."

"I'm glad. I thought she was perfect for you."

"Thank you for thinking of it," Nina says. "She makes me feel like I already have a friend here."

"Two friends," I remind her. "Don't forget about me."

"There's no possible way I could do that." We stop before walking into the parlor where my parents are waiting, and I lean down to lay a simple kiss on Nina's cheek, reassuring us both.

"Here goes nothing, darling."

We walk into the room, and I'm immediately surprised to see not only my parents but also all three of my siblings.

Nina's hand tightens on my arm.

"Hello, everyone." We stop in front of them all, and they stand. I start with my parents. "Mum, Father, I'd like to introduce you to Nina Wolfe."

To my utter fascination and delight, Nina executes a perfect curtsy and smiles genuinely at my father. "It's a pleasure to meet you, Your Majesty."

She then turns to my mother and offers her the same greeting.

My mum's eyes turn to mine in surprise before she leans in to kiss Nina's cheek.

"It's a pleasure to meet you, Nina."

"My turn," Callum says. "I'm the best-looking brother. Callum."

"Your Royal Highness." Nina curtsies again.

I introduce her to my sister Eleanor, along with my brother Frederick and his wife, Catherine.

Once the introductions are finished, Nina and I sit in uncomfortable chairs, facing the others as if we're in a job interview.

Because, of course, we are.

"I trust your travels were pleasant," Father begins. He hasn't broken a smile.

"Yes, thank you," I reply.

"How did you meet?" Eleanor asks, breaking the uncomfortable silence.

"She ran into me. Literally."

"On accident," Nina clarifies and smiles. "I didn't see him there."

"And then you got her number?" Callum asks.

"No, she wouldn't give it to me."

Everyone's eyebrows climb, making me laugh.

"I was taught not to give my phone number to strangers," Nina says with a shrug. "Even handsome ones."

"Especially handsome ones," Catherine says and winks.

"Then I saw her later that night in a restaurant. I still didn't get her number, but we have a mutual friend. Jacob," I add and take Nina's hand in mine. "And he told me where she lives."

"He showed up the next morning while I was out on the lake on my boat. I have a lake house. And I asked him if the royal family was aware that they have a stalker on their hands."

This actually makes everyone laugh. My father even smiles, which shocks the hell out of me.

"I can't say he's ever been arrested for stalking," Mum says.

"I couldn't resist her," I say and kiss her knuckles. "She's obviously beautiful, but more than that, she's a challenge. And an intelligent one at that."

"She snagged herself a prince, didn't she?" Father asks, speaking for the first time.

"I think I'm here *despite* that fact," Nina says before I can reply. "I mean no offense, of course. My background is in publicity. My brother is Christian Wolfe, the actor—"

"Oh, he's *hot*," Eleanor murmurs, earning a glare from Mum.

"—and I've worked as his public relations manager for close to a decade. I know what it is to be scrutinized every step you take. I've always counted my blessings that it wasn't *me* in that spotlight. At least not at the same level as my brother. So, when Sebastian asked me to marry him, I had to consider that and give it a great deal of thought."

"And yet, here you are," my brother Frederick says.

"Here I am." She looks up at me and offers me a wide smile. "I don't think I've ever known anyone quite like your brother."

"Your ring is quite beautiful," Mum says, gesturing to the diamond on Nina's finger. "Who made it?"

"A goldsmith in Montana," I reply. "He's well known in the area, and his work is impeccable."

"It's lovely," Catherine adds.

"It will be replaced, of course," Mum says.

Nina looks down at her ring with a frown. "I quite love this ring."

"It should be a piece from the vault," Eleanor explains kindly. "It's tradition."

"She'll wear what she has for a while yet," my father says firmly. "Until we've decided that she's staying, she'll keep the new ring."

I glare at my father. "That's not the way I was taught to treat guests."

"I've never suggested giving the royal jewels to guests," he says. "Until she has my blessing, she won't be in the vault."

"I'm happy with this ring," Nina insists, looking up at me with pleading blue eyes that say, *"just drop it."*

For her sake, I will. For now.

"When do you plan to marry?" Callum asks.

"Next week," I reply.

"Absolutely not," Mum says, shaking her head. "I won't have it. There is protocol, and you'll give us the proper amount of time to plan a suitable wedding."

"Mum—"

"I will not budge on this," she insists. "You're asking us to accept quite a lot here, Sebastian. The least you can do is compromise and let us plan this wedding correctly."

I glance down at Nina. She's already nodding. "It's the right thing to do."

"How much time do you need?" I ask Mum.

"Six months, at least."

"I'll give you six weeks."

She starts to argue, but I shake my head. "Six weeks, or we elope next week. The choice is yours."

"Why are you in such a hurry?" Frederick asks.

"Because his birthday is in a few weeks," Father replies.

"Because I love her." I hold my father's gaze firmly. "It has nothing to do with my birthday or the ridiculous law. I love her, and I want to be with her. End of story."

"Well, I think it's romantic," Eleanor says, jumping up to throw her arms around Nina in a hug. "I'm happy you're here. If you need anything at all, just ask."

"Mary's working with her," I say and watch as Eleanor lights up even more.

"Oh, that's brilliant. Mary's perfect."

"I'd like you all to leave so I can have a word with my son." My father watches me as the others do as he wishes.

"I'll walk you back to Sebastian's quarters," Eleanor offers, taking Nina's hand in hers. "We'll have a chat. Oh, this is so exciting!"

Once we're alone, my father and I sit in silence for about twenty seconds. I wait for him to start.

"Do you understand what this means?" he asks at last.

"Perfectly."

"You have a duty to Great Britain—"

"I know what my duty is," I interrupt, surprising him. "It's been ingrained in me from birth."

"And yet you do this."

I pinch the bridge of my nose and take a deep breath.

"I know you've never listened to me because it's not what you wanted to hear, but I've been telling you for years that I don't want to be king. I never have, Father."

"We don't get to choose!" His voice rises in agitation, which is unusual for him. He's typically just cold. "We're born into this, chosen by God himself. Who do you think you are, to go against God's wishes?"

"I'm a human being," I remind him. "With free will. I *love* my country and its people. I am blessed to be a part of this family, and I hope you don't shun me and shuttle me off to France or somewhere else. I love the crown. I am British. But, Father, I don't believe that I'd make a good king. I'm a good man, but that doesn't necessarily translate to being a good monarch. I'm happy to continue my work. I've completed almost a decade in the military, and I have many causes that I want to continue working for. I have so much good to do.

"But being crowned the king isn't in my future. Frederick will make an excellent ruler, and you know it."

Father sighs and rubs his fingertips over his forehead.

"I'm sorry that I'm a disappointment. An embarrassment."

"Stop." His gaze flies to mine again. "I am disappointed, yes. But never embarrassed. You *are* a good man, and I think you underestimate yourself."

I stare at him in absolute shock. I've never heard those words come from my father's mouth. He's not a warm parent.

"But if this is what you truly want, if she is who you love, I'll allow it. I still don't like it, Sebastian. You can't expect me to. I have decisions to make where you're concerned because of the choices you made. Difficult ones."

"I'm asking you not to shun me."

He's quiet for a long moment. "I couldn't live with myself if I did that. But I have to read the laws and decide if you will retain your title. And what title, if any, Nina will hold. There's protocol here, son."

"I understand."

"I hope you do. You've just managed to change the course of the royal family forever. The history books, the lines of succession. Everything."

"Yes, sir." I nod, suddenly feeling like a weight

has been lifted off my chest. He's going to agree to this. For the first time in my life, I'm free to be a regular citizen.

Or closer to it anyway.

"I have things to see to," Father says and stands. I join him and wait as he leaves the room, then I set off in the opposite direction to find Nina.

We need to celebrate.

CHAPTER 6

I SURE HOPE we don't have to go anywhere else this evening because I've already changed out of my dress and into a tank and yoga pants.

I may not be allowed to wear pants in public, but in the privacy of our home, I'll be wearing these comfortable nuggets of amazingness.

Please, God, let him tell me I can wear yoga pants at home.

I've just pulled my hair into a high ponytail and washed my face clean when I hear the door open. Hoping it's *not* a member of the royal staff, I poke my head around the corner and smile when I see it's Sebastian.

He's my fiancé.

Holy shit.

"Hey," I say and walk into the living room. "How did that go?"

He blows out a breath and props his hands on his hips, watching me thoughtfully. "Better than I expected."

"That's…good?"

"Yes, it's good. You look so young dressed like that."

I smile and turn a little circle for him. "Please tell me I can wear this when we're here in your apartment. I'll wear skirts and dresses every day, but when we're here, this is how I get comfortable."

"You can wear whatever you like in here," he confirms. "In fact, I'll join you."

He turns and walks into his bedroom, stripping out of his tie on the way. I hear him rustling around, and about five minutes later, he's back wearing an Oxford T-shirt and a pair of basketball shorts.

"Wow, you're really casual."

"I have my moments."

I'm sitting on the couch with my legs pulled up under me, relaxing. "Aren't you tired?"

"To the bone," he confirms and sits next to me on the chaise side of the couch, stretching out his legs. "It feels like this is the day that will never end."

"It's been eventful," I agree.

"Would you like some dinner?"

"Do you have room service in the palace?"

"Of course, we do." He reaches over for my hand and rubs his thumb across my knuckles. "You can have anything you want, any time of day."

"It's like a really fancy Four Seasons." I take stock of my body. "But I'm not ready for food yet. I think I'm too jet-lagged."

"Tired?"

"Hmm. I know it's like eight here, but it's only noon back home, and I feel like I could sleep for a week."

"Come here." He crooks a finger, inviting me to snuggle with him.

I have never been a snuggler.

But I said *no* to and about a lot of things before I met Sebastian. Maybe me trying new things is a trend.

I scoot over and lay right on top of him, my head resting on his chest, my arms wrapped around him, our legs tangled.

He's firm and warm, and his arms are strong as they loop around me. I don't know that I ever felt better than I do right here and now.

He kisses the top of my head, and I sigh deeply. Oh, yeah, this is great. I could fall asleep right here.

"Am I squishing you?" I ask.

"No, darling," he says softly. My tank has ridden up, and his hand lands on the small of my back. He draws light circles with his fingertips.

Damn, that feels good.

I can't help it. I press a kiss to his chest and then nuzzle his impressive pec muscles, enjoying the way he feels beneath me.

The circles on my lower back turn into caresses, running up my spine under my tank, and then back down again. When he pushes his hand under my yoga pants to cup my bare ass beneath, I have to hold back a moan.

Sebastian has the best hands in the world.

But instead of putting me to sleep, he's awakening my body, making my heartbeat speed up.

"Nina," he whispers as he guides me, lying me on the couch lengthwise before covering me with his body. "You're incredible."

"Likewise."

His lips twitch before he covers my mouth with his, kissing me with lazy heat. He's in no hurry, but he's as turned on as I am. When he settles his hips in the cradle of my pelvis, his arousal is obvious.

And pressing against me.

Good God, he's impressive.

He pushes my shirt up and latches onto a nipple

as I take the tank off and drop it onto the floor. I arch my back, longing for more.

Give me more.

"You're absolutely beautiful," he mutters as he switches from one hard and wet nipple to the other. His hands are *everywhere.* Roaming down my side to my hip before he pushes one amazing hand under the waistband of my pants to find my core. "And you're not wearing any knickers."

"No knickers for this girl," I say with a grin. "If that means underwear."

"It does." He kisses down my sternum to my navel and hangs out there for a long moment, circling my belly button with his nose before leaving wet kisses down to my pubis. He pulls off my pants, tosses them aside, and opens me wide, looking his fill. "Bloody hell."

"You have *way* too many clothes on," I remind him, reaching for him, but he dodges out of my way. His usually tidy dark blond hair is mussed from my fingers, and his eyes are ice-blue as he takes me in from head to toe. No one has ever looked at me with the kind of lust that's coming from Sebastian right now.

So, this is what the fuss is all about.

"You first." With that, he licks me from clit to opening and back again, and I'm lost to him. I grip the edge of the couch, fisting my hand as my toes curl. As if that weren't enough, he plunges two fingers inside of me, and I'm lost. My legs start to shake. Light explodes behind my eyelids.

This is how I die.

But what a way to go.

"Oh, God." My back arches again, and everything...*everything* explodes around me. Through me.

If this is heaven, I don't want to be resuscitated.

"I'm dead."

Sebastian chuckles as he kisses up my stomach, then my sternum, and settles in to kiss me slowly on the mouth again. He brushes the hair off my cheeks and nips my chin.

"I've wanted to do that for what feels like forever."

"Three days."

"Longest three days of my bloody life."

He stands and lifts me into his arms. I loop my arms around his neck.

"Where are we going?"

"To bed."

"Mine or yours?"

"It's ours now," he says, frowning down at me.

"I have my own room. I thought I'd be sleeping in there."

"Fuck that." I raise an eyebrow. "You have your own space, yes, but you'll be sleeping with *me*. This is our bed, and I'll have you in it."

"Bossy," I murmur, dragging my finger down his cheek. "But I like it."

He lowers me to the cool linens covering the ridiculously soft mattress. The bed's already been turned down.

I bet the sheets are at least a thousand thread count.

I have a thing for good sheets.

But rather than discuss the palace's choice in linens, I reach for Sebastian's shirt and pull it over his head, tossing it aside.

"Whoa," I whisper before I can control myself.

"Is that a good whoa, or a bad one?"

"Have you *seen* you? My God, you look like you've been sculpted. Or photoshopped."

"I train," he says simply, peppering kisses over my shoulder. "And have you seen *you*?"

"Are we going to spend the whole night dishing out compliments? Or are we going to get to the good stuff?"

He smiles down at me. "What kind of good stuff?"

"You know." I let my hand wander down his ridiculously hard abs and over his shorts, cupping his hard cock in my palm. "It involves this."

"Oh, yes. We'll be getting to the good stuff."

I help him out of his shorts, and when we're finally and blissfully naked together, Sebastian surprises me by simply tipping his forehead against mine and holding me close.

"This isn't the good stuff I was talking about."

He smiles. "I'm just taking my time, darling. I'm enjoying you."

"There's no need for that."

He frowns now. "Why the hell not?"

I shrug a shoulder and look away, but he catches my chin in his fingers and pulls my focus back to him.

"I'm used to fast and fun and then going our separate ways," I admit.

"Oh, Nina." He kisses my lips, just barely touching them. "That's not how this is going to go at all. Just trust me."

No more words are needed. He sets to methodically making me crazy. His hands, those amazing freaking hands, are on a mission to drive me insane. He plucks my nipple, then soothes it with his tongue. He drags his blunt nails up my side from my ass to my breast. His touch is firmer now, but he's not moving faster.

Damn it, I want him inside of me!

I loop my leg up around his hip in invitation, but rather than sink in, he just uses his hand and brings me to a climax that might rival the eruption of Mt. St. Helens.

I was right, he's going to kill me.

"Sebastian."

"What do you need?"

"You." It's a sob now. I'm not proud of it, but I can't stop it. "Please, I just need you."

There's rustling, the tear of a packet, and then he finally, *finally* covers me once more, cradling my head in his hands as he sinks slowly into my heat.

"Jesus, Nina."

Once he's seated as far as he can go, he stops to kiss me, long and hard. Finally, his hips begin to move in long and smooth strokes.

"You're hitting just the right spot," I mutter before biting his arm and clenching around him. I come so quickly, it takes us both by surprise.

I thought for sure it would take a while to build back up, especially after two orgasms.

I was wrong.

"Good girl." He begins moving faster, much harder. "You amaze me. I can't keep my hands off of you."

"Good. Don't keep them off me." I grip his ass,

urging him to go harder. Deeper.

To my delight, he falls over the edge into his own orgasm, his eyes pinned to mine as he goes.

It's been a solid week of being in the palace. And by that, I mean I've literally not left the palace grounds since the day Sebastian and I walked in a week ago.

There hasn't been time to breathe, much less get out to see London.

I've spent my days with Mary, learning everything from family history to how to behave in public. I'm not allowed to kiss Sebastian. I am allowed to hold his hand. I must sit with my ankles crossed, never my knees.

The way I speak, the way I must school my face, *everything* is given as a rule.

It's fascinating and disconcerting all at the same time.

When I'm not training with Mary, I'm with a seamstress who is literally building a wardrobe around my body. I mean, I knew that they wouldn't buy my clothes off a rack, but I had no idea that the garments would be made especially for me.

The clothes are beautiful. And for the most part, the staff is kind. I see the side-eye that some of them give me, and I'm sure they talk amongst themselves, but they're discreet and smart enough to know that they'd better not get caught.

I've barely seen Sebastian this week. We spend breakfast together each morning, but then he's gone all day. I see him at dinner, and we spend each night together, having the craziest sex of my life.

It's not so bad. I just wish I had more time with him during the day. I like Mary very much, but it's not the same.

There's a knock on the door to the apartment, and I answer it to find Nick, my new personal security guard, standing on the other side.

"Your presence has been requested at afternoon tea with the queen and Princess Eleanor," he says formally.

"Oh, thank you. I'll be ready in a moment."

I need to change into a suitable dress for afternoon tea with the royal women. I still can't help but ponder why on Earth I need a personal bodyguard.

I haven't left the palace in a week.

It's not like I need to be escorted here and there.

But I don't question much. If the royal family wants to pay some poor guy to follow me around with no danger in sight, so be it.

Once I've changed and quickly brushed my hair, I join Nick in the hallway.

"I'm ready."

He nods once and then leads the way to the room I was in when I first met Sebastian's family. But rather than a whole audience, today it's just Her Majesty and Eleanor.

"Hello, Nina," the queen says. I offer her a curtsy.

"Your Majesty. Your Highness."

"Please, have a seat." The queen gestures to the chair beside Eleanor. "Thank you for joining us."

"Thank you for inviting me."

A servant pours my tea, adding sugar and milk just the way I like it. It's amazing to me how fast the staff has learned my likes and dislikes.

It's as if they're all robots and they've been programmed.

I've only spent two dinners with the family since that first introduction. And I've quickly learned that just because we all live in the same giant building, it doesn't mean we see much of each other.

"How are you settling in?" Eleanor asks, nibbling on a finger sandwich.

"Nicely, I think." I sip my tea. "It's been a busy week."

"It's about to get busier," the queen says with a kind smile. "We have some wedding plans to make. I've already spoken with the event planner, and preparations are underway, but there are many things that, as a bride, you need to be involved with."

I stare at her, suddenly terrified. I know that nearly every girl in the world has planned her wedding from the time she was roughly six.

But not me.

Because I never thought to get married.

"You look like you've seen a ghost," Eleanor says with a laugh. "This is the fun part. You get to choose flowers and colors and *your dress.*"

"Oh, boy."

"I didn't mean to overwhelm you," the queen says, narrowing her eyes. "Aren't you excited about your wedding?"

Not in the least.

"Of course," I assure them both. "Of course, I am. It's just a lot to take in. Everyone has already been so kind and accommodating. It's more than I expected."

"You're marrying a prince," Eleanor reminds me. "It's definitely a lot to take in. Catherine felt the same way when she married Frederick, and they had a seven-month engagement."

"We're here to help," the queen says kindly. "We enjoy this sort of thing very much."

"Thank you. Truly."

I sigh and take another sip of tea.

"Nina, I don't mean this to sound unkind, but you look quite exhausted."

"I am," I admit. "It's been such a busy week that I haven't even left the palace since I arrived."

"You need a break," Eleanor says with a nod.

"Why don't you two go to the spa?" the queen asks. "I'm quite sure the Ritz can take you for a few hours. Have some champagne, get pampered a bit. Relax."

"Oh, that sounds lovely," Eleanor says, turning to me. "Nina?"

"Yes, please. That does sound lovely."

"Wonderful. I'll arrange it right now." The queen signals her assistant, who immediately pulls a cell phone out of her bag and starts making calls.

"They can see you in forty-five minutes," she says.

"Lovely," the queen replies with a smile. "Have a wonderful time, girls."

"Good God, I needed that." I clink my glass to El-lie's and smile over at her. Now that we've been naked together and are a little buzzed, she insisted that we cut the formalities.

"Me, too. I have to go to Scotland tomorrow on

official business, and this is a great way to charge my batteries before the trip."

"I have to plan a wedding." I stare down into my glass. "I don't know what to choose."

"Anything you choose will be lovely," Ellie says with a smile. "And we have event people to help steer you in the right direction."

I glance over as Nick and Philip, Ellie's bodyguard, talk amongst themselves.

"Do you ever get used to having security with you all the time?"

"I don't know." She sips her bubbly. "I've always had it. And can I just say, that new guy? Nick? He's *so* handsome."

I look at the man again and shrug. He's no Sebastian.

"I'll give you that. Tall, dark, and handsome with a strong chin is never a horrible combination."

"I wouldn't mind having *him* guard my body," she says, making us both giggle.

"I think this champagne is going to my head."

"That and the incredible massage and facials," she agrees. "But so worth it."

I nod. These few hours were nice, but I'm ready to get back to Sebastian, to tell him all about my afternoon.

We finish our drinks and then walk into the

locker room where we change back into our dresses. Soon, we're whisked back to the palace.

"Thanks for going with me," I say to Ellie as I give her a hug just inside the palace doors. "I had a great time."

"Me, too. We'll do it again." She smiles brightly before stumbling off toward her own living quarters. I walk in the opposite direction, to Sebastian's apartment. I'm nearly there when my heel catches on the rug, and I pitch forward. Nick catches me just before I fall on my face.

"Easy there," he says.

I laugh and brace my hand on his chest as I right myself.

"Thanks. I guess you're good for something, after all."

He smiles, just as the door of the apartment opens and Sebastian walks out of it.

"What in the hell is going on?"

CHAPTER 7

Sebastian

I NEVER UNDERSTOOD the term *seeing red* until this moment.

Nick has his arms around Nina, and she's smiling up at him as if they're sharing an intimate joke between lovers.

And that is *not* okay.

"Sir," Nick says, clearing his throat. "I just stopped her from falling."

"I don't know why I'm such a klutz. Thanks, Nick." She walks to me, smiling happily. "Hey there, handsome prince."

"That'll be all," I say to Nick, dismissing him and leading Nina into my flat, closing the door behind us. When we're alone, I turn to her, anger and other emotions I'm not comfortable labeling coursing through me. "What the hell was that all about?"

She sits on the couch and frowns up at me. "What?"

"That." I gesture to the hallway. "You and Nick in a bloody embrace."

She blinks slowly as if she's trying to understand what I'm saying.

"Am I speaking English? Because I can use a different language if you're more comfortable."

"Don't speak to me like that," she says softly. "You may be royalty, but you don't get to belittle me. Today or any day."

"I apologize."

"I had too much champagne." She rubs her temple. "And a fabulous massage. So I was clumsy, and Nick caught me before I plowed face-first into that five-hundred-year-old table and took my teeth out."

I cross my arms over my chest, watching her quietly. I was going out of my mind not able to find her. I didn't know where she went.

Only to find her in the arms of her bodyguard.

"You look mad."

"Frustrated," I reply. "Where were you?"

"I went to the spa with Ellie." I raise a brow at the use of my sister's nickname. Only those closest to her get to call her that. "And we had a blissful few hours that didn't include being here in the palace."

"Do you hate it here?"

"No, of course not. But I haven't left in a week, Sebastian. I just needed a break."

Of course. I'm a bloody idiot.

"And your mother, who I think likes me by the way, suggested that Ellie and I go to the spa. It was really nice."

"I'm glad." I sit across from her and drag my hand down my face. "I'm sorry for behaving like a buffoon."

"A buffoon?" She grins. "You say the funniest things."

"You are a bit pissed, aren't you?"

She nods and bites her lip, then crosses over to me and climbs into my lap.

I wrap my arms around her and bury my face into her neck. "I couldn't find you. I came back here to have dinner with you, and you weren't here."

"I'm sorry." She brushes her fingers through my hair, and I'm immediately calmer.

"Why didn't you answer your mobile?"

"I turned it off three days ago."

"What? Why?"

She sighs and lays her head on my shoulder.

"Because I used to be Christian's publicist. Which means most media outlets have my number."

"Fuck." I kiss her head. "You're being bombarded."

"Pretty much. So, I check it once a day to message Christian and make sure my mom's okay, and then I turn it off again. Christian has Mary's number if there's an emergency."

"I'm so sorry, darling. We can change your number."

"I know, and I will. But I've had enough going on. It's really not that big of a deal."

She burrows deeper against me. She insists that she doesn't like to be touched, but we've touched constantly this past week when we're together.

I don't want to point it out. I'm afraid she'll stop.

I enjoy her.

"I have a surprise for you tomorrow."

Her head comes up with that announcement. "Really? What?"

"If I tell you, it's not a surprise."

"I hate surprises." She kisses my chin. "Please, tell me."

"We're going away for a couple of days. You need a change of scenery, and I need to catch my breath. I've been buried in work this past week."

"Is everything okay?" She cups my face, and I turn my head to kiss her palm.

"It is. Let's just get away together for a little while."

"That sounds nice."

"This is your idea of a cottage?"

We're standing beside the car, looking at our country home. It's a tall, stone building that's stood through many wars.

It's my favorite place.

"This is actually Craigowan Lodge," I reply with a smile. "It's much smaller than a castle."

"Yes. It's tiny." Her voice is as dry as the Sahara Desert, which only makes me laugh.

"Trust me, compared to the castle about a mile away, this is small. It only has seven bedrooms."

"How ever shall we survive?" she asks, batting her eyelashes.

We spend the morning getting settled. The building may be five hundred years old, but it's been updated to be modern, with all of the comforts a royal family could want.

"Let's go ride the horses," I suggest, leaning my shoulder on the doorjamb as I watch her brush her hair. She whisks it up into a ponytail and turns to me with pleading eyes.

"*Please* tell me I can wear pants for this. I will not get on a horse in a skirt."

"Of course, you can." I kiss her nose and then pat her bottom. "Hurry and change. I'm anxious to get outside."

"Right behind you," she assures me as I leave the room and head down to the kitchen, where the cook is putting together a basket that smells delicious.

"I've made you plenty to keep your bellies full," he assures me. "It's good to see you, sir."

"And you." I shake his hand and thank him for the food. "We'll be back in time for dinner."

"Excellent. I'm making lamb."

"I can't wait."

Nina hurries down to join me, and we walk out to the stable where Charles and Nick are already preparing the horses.

"You're ready," Charles says. "Nick and I will be behind you, should anything happen."

"Nothing's going to happen," I reply. "We're in the country, and no one knows we're here."

"We'll be with you all the same, sir," Charles replies. He's still angry about Montana and won't let me out of his sight.

It's bloody annoying.

I help Nina up into her saddle, and then I mount my own horse. We set off, trotting through the trees and pastures.

"This area is beautiful," Nina says. "How old is Craigowan Lodge?"

"Are you sure you want this history lesson?"

"Absolutely. Show me how smart you are." She winks at me, and I make a mental note to spank her perky arse later.

"That particular building has been in existence since approximately sixteen-fifty."

Her eyes round as she looks over to me. "Wow."

"Darling, we have castles more than nine hundred years old."

"Wow again."

"We'll ride past some ruins today that go back to the thirteen-hundreds. Monarchs such as King Robert II of Scotland used this area as a hunting lodge."

"That's incredible. We don't have anything this old in the States. Not really. Our history just doesn't go back that far."

"I could bore you for weeks with the history I know about this area. It always fascinated me. I loved coming here in the summer with my family. We ran around these woods like wild children, getting dirty and truly playing. We had to be much more civilized at the palace in London."

"At least you got to play," she says. "And what a beautiful area to spend time in."

"It's still used as a vacation house, and guests stay here, as well. Some of the Russian monarchy spend time here."

"Why?"

"They're all related," I say with a shrug.

"Even the Russians?"

"A hundred years ago, the Russian czar married a German princess. *And* he was a cousin of King George."

"I had no idea," she breathes. "You can give me history lessons anytime you want. It's fascinating."

"Be careful what you wish for." I lead us to a clearing with a massive and ancient tree that offers some shade. "Let's stop here, let the horses rest, and eat a bite, shall we?"

"We shall." She grins and slides off her horse.

"You know how to ride."

"I do," she agrees. "My mom set Christian and me up with lessons outside of L.A. when we were kids. I think it was her way of getting rid of us for a week in the summer."

"Do you like to ride?"

"I could take it or leave it. Tomorrow, when my

ass and thighs are sore, I'll want to leave it. But I do like seeing places like these that I wouldn't be able to get to otherwise, so I'm happy to be doing this with you today. The fresh air is nice."

"I'm sorry you've been so cooped up at the palace this past week." I spread the blanket out and set the basket of food in the middle of it. Charles and Nick are eating their own lunch, far enough away that we can't hear what they're talking about.

I'm glad. I want this time with Nina, away from my family and security. It's like we're back in our bubble again.

"I really can't complain, Sebastian. It's not like I'm being held in a dungeon. I have a beautiful apartment, in the most luxurious private home in the world."

"Still, I know you're used to doing as you please, and this is an adjustment."

"For both of us. This hasn't been easy on you, either."

I want to pull her to me and kiss the hell out of her. I love that she sees this, knows me well enough in such a short time to know that I haven't had a great week either.

But I pass her the lunch the cook prepared, and we eat in companionable silence, listening to the birds.

"Sometimes, I think there are ghosts here," I

admit and take another bite of my sandwich. "How can there not be, after so much time? Battles were fought here, babies born. A lot of life has happened."

"Oh, it's absolutely haunted," she agrees quickly. "And while I don't exactly want to see Marie Antoinette holding her head, I think it's pretty cool."

"Marie Antoinette was French, darling."

"You know what I mean."

"We have a lot to teach you." I set my sandwich aside, hers as well, and then lean in to kiss her. I don't care that Charles and Nick are nearby. I can't resist her.

"Me getting your history wrong turns you on?"

"*You* turn me on." I nibble her plump lips and push her back onto the blanket. My hand finds its way under her shirt.

"People are watching."

"If they know what's good for them, they've gone to find something else to do." I glance up and, sure enough, Charles and Nick have walked away. "See? They're gone."

"Good." She sinks her fingers into my hair and pulls me down to her, kissing me for all she's worth. She's bloody intoxicating.

I never stop wanting her. I want her *now*, out

here in the open, but I know it's not safe. Someone could come upon us at any time.

So I slowly back away, kissing her cheek and then her nose as I do.

"We should head back."

"Thank God, because that's where the bed is."

"I like the way you think, darling."

"Oh, crap!"

I spin at Nina's yelp in time to see Nick wrapping his arms around her waist and plucking her foot out of the stirrup.

We just returned to the stables, and I was busy taking the saddle off my horse.

It seems Nick is taking my girl off of hers.

"Are you all right?" I ask, rushing to her.

"Oh, yeah," she says with a laugh. "My foot got caught. Nick rescued me."

I give the other man a hard look, silently telling him to back the bloody hell off, which he does immediately. I tuck Nina against my side and lead her inside, then through the house up to our bedroom.

"I'm going to let you freshen up, darling. I'll be back in a few moments."

"Okay. I need a shower after that ride."

I'd love to join her, but I have something else to see to.

I return downstairs and find Charles with Nick in the drawing room.

"Charles, I'd like a word."

He nods at Nick, who hurries from the room, shutting the double doors behind him.

"What's on your mind, sir?"

"Nick is on my mind." I can hear the ice in my voice. "I want him replaced by someone else."

"That's impossible, sir."

I cock a brow. "The correct answer is 'yes, sir.'"

Charles sighs and shakes his head. "I'm sorry, Your Highness, but Nick is the best man I have on staff right now. All of my extra men are still in Cunningham Falls."

I push my hand through my hair and pace away from him.

"He's too *hands-on*," I say and point toward the stable. "That's the second time in as many days that I've caught him touching her."

"She was going to fall," Charles says. "Both times. He reported it to me, Sebastian. Are you jealous because he's a young, handsome man and you think he'll steal her from you?"

"Watch yourself."

"He has no interest in Nina in any other way than as a client. He's signed contracts that outline what will happen to his position should he cross that line."

"I don't like it."

Charles is quiet as he watches me, and then he pours each of us a snifter of brandy. I take the glass and drink it in one swallow.

"Perhaps you should have this conversation with Nick."

"I'd likely punch him, and that's not good employer-employee relations."

Charles turns to me in surprise. "I've never known you to be a jealous man."

"You've never known me with Nina. There has to be *someone* who can be assigned to her."

"Nick is the best man on my staff. If you love her the way you say you do, you'll want her to have the best."

I glare at him, my whole body quaking in anger and frustration.

"Bugger me." I turn on my heel and stomp out of the room.

I don't have to pretend that I'm in love with her. I'm already halfway there.

"I don't want to get up," Nina murmurs the next morning. We're snuggled down in the bed, listening to the rain batter the roof above us. "It's just too nice here."

"We could have a lie-in, we don't have to get up for a while yet." She's pressed against me, her bottom snuggled tightly against my groin, facing the window. I'm already hard.

It seems I'm constantly hard when she's near.

"I didn't know that rain could sound so beautiful." She wiggles onto her back and smiles up at me, dragging her fingers down my cheek. "This is the perfect day to stay under the covers and have sex all day long."

"Now, that's tempting." I nibble the side of her lips and down to her jawline. "You smell so good. What is that?"

"Soap." She laughs and then sighs when I cup her breast, tweaking the nipple between my fingers. "Oh, that's nice. Have I mentioned you're really good with your hands?"

"I don't think so."

"*So good.*" She arches into my touch. She's still warm from sleep, her movements slow and groggy.

She's blooming gorgeous.

Before I can move over her, she straddles my hips, impaling herself completely. Her head falls back, and I can't resist sitting up to bite her neck, her collarbone.

"Can't get enough of you," I growl as she begins to move. My hands grip her hips, my fingertips digging into her arse as she rides me.

"I'm so sore from riding the horses yesterday," she says with a laugh. I wrap my arm around her waist and switch our positions, kissing her as I begin to move now. I link my fingers with hers and pin her hand above her head. Her other hand digs into my backside.

"You're strong," she whispers. "I like it."

I can't speak. The orgasm has begun to gather in my spine, working its way through me. I move faster, grinding against her core, wanting her to join me.

"Shit," she whispers, the first contractions coming from her core. She's tugging and squeezing me, and all control is gone as I let go, spilling myself inside her.

Holy bloody hell.

"Nina."

"Mmm. That was nice."

"Nina, I didn't wear a rubber. Shite, I'm so sorry."

Her eyes spring open, but she just kisses the inside of my arm. "We're good, Prince Sebastian.

No baby princes will be made today."

"This isn't funny."

She cups my cheeks and looks into my eyes. "I have an IUD. I promise, I can't get pregnant. And I'm perfectly healthy."

I blow out a gusty breath and tip my forehead against hers. "So daft. I've never lost my mind like that before."

"I'll take it as a compliment." She grabs my arse again. "You were too excited to fuck me to remember the condom."

"I don't *fuck* you, darling." I nibble her lips to keep myself from telling her that I'm making love to her. "Never that."

"I know." She sighs in contentment. "Trust me, you've shown me the difference."

"What a lovely thing to say." I move to the side and bring her with me, snuggling her to me so we can lay in bed and listen to the rain.

"It's true. But if you tell anyone else, I'll deny it."

"It's our secret."

CHAPTER 8

Nina

"YOU'RE GETTING MARRIED in a week!" Fallon runs to me and throws her arms around me, hugging me tightly. "And you said you'd never marry. Famous last words."

It's *so good* to see my friends. Christian and Jenna arrived last week, and just this morning, the rest of the gang flew in. Fallon and Noah, Willa and Max, Hannah and Brad, and of course, Grace and Jacob.

I have my whole tribe around me for the first time in over a month. To say I feel relieved is a gross understatement. I want to kiss them all on the mouth.

Me, the one who doesn't like to be touched.

"I can't believe we're in the palace," Hannah

murmurs into my ear as she hugs me. "How are you? You look healthy. Should I do a quick examination while I'm here?"

"She's in England, not a third-world country," Grace reminds her with a grin. "But really, though. How are you?"

"Overwhelmed," I admit and blink away tears. "It's just been a lot, you know? But I can't complain because it's also amazing. And holy shit, you guys, I'm marrying a prince."

"A freaking *prince*," Willa says with a grin. "I want to see your wardrobe. I *need* access to your closet."

"Done," I say immediately. "Where are the guys?"

"Sebastian already scooped them all up and took them fox hunting for the day," Jenna says with a smile.

"Hunting?" I ask and frown at Fallon. "I don't think Noah will be on board with that."

"He's from Montana," Fallon replies with a shrug. "Hunting is a thing there. But if there are any injured birds, he can help."

"Hello, everyone," Eleanor says with a smile. "Catherine and I are here to take everyone to the spa for the day."

Jenna gives Eleanor a high-five, surprising me.

In the week that Jenna and Christian have been here, they've grown to really like Sebastian's family. And, to my delight, the family seems to like them in return.

It's been an awesome week.

"I could seriously use a massage after that flight," Grace says. "I had no idea that a red-eye could be so exhausting. I thought I'd sleep on the plane."

"No sleep?" I ask.

"Not even a little," Willa says. "None of us slept. Well, except Max, who can sleep anywhere."

"Well then, the spa is the perfect way to freshen up," Catherine says with a kind smile. I haven't spent much time with Catherine. She and Frederick took their children to another home in Scotland for a month, so they've been away from the palace most of the time I've been here.

"Shall we go?" Eleanor asks.

"Let's go," I say.

"So, basically, I could live in your closet," Willa says much later after we've all been to the spa and back again. We decided to continue the party in my apartment.

"It's the size of your house in Montana," Fallon says, sipping her champagne. "You have more shoes than I've ever seen."

"I spent weeks being fitted for all of these clothes," I reply. "Do you have any idea how hard it is to stand in one place for hours at a time and not get stuck by pins?"

"We do," Eleanor says with a laugh. "And it's quite tedious."

"It's the worst," Catherine agrees. "Tell us about your home in Montana."

"It's on the lake," I begin and smile as I think about my little house. "I have a boat, and I love being out on the water."

"It's her happy place," Fallon adds.

"But this isn't a bad trade," Grace says thoughtfully. "Also, I'm *so* happy I can drink champagne again."

"You had a baby earlier this year, didn't you?" Catherine asks. "I only know that because Sebastian is so close to Jacob, and he told us all the news."

"It's such a small world," Hannah says.

"I did. And now I can *finally* celebrate things with my friends again with a glass of champagne or wine. Don't get me wrong, I adore my daughter, but sometimes, a girl needs a drink."

"I understand," Catherine replies. She's a beautiful woman with auburn hair and brown eyes. "I have two children myself."

Grace and Catherine sit in the living room, talking all about babies and kids. Ellie and Jenna are trying on my shoes.

Willa and Hannah follow me to the kitchen, where I pull out platters of food from the fridge.

"None of this was here earlier," I say in surprise.

"I had it brought in," Ellie says. "Or I asked my assistant to have it brought in. I figured we would want to go somewhere private for some girl-time."

"Thank you."

A knock on the door surprises me. When I open it, Nick announces, "Her Majesty, the queen."

We all immediately curtsy as she walks into the room. When the door is shut, she just smiles, looking around the space.

"Oh, isn't this wonderful? May I please have a glass of champagne?"

The Queen of freaking England just crashed my bachelorette party.

"Of course." I pour her a glass and pass it to her. Then, to my utter surprise, she takes my hand in hers and holds on tightly.

I haven't had nearly enough alcohol for this.

Or maybe I've had too much. I'll surely say the

wrong thing.

"I know it hasn't been easy," she begins. "Trust me, I understand. Although I am British by birth, I was not born to an affluent family. It was all a culture shock to me when my husband asked me to marry him.

"I want to tell you that I think you're lovely. And I also think that despite not being British, you are a good match for my son. He smiles easier since you've been here. He seems happy. And at the end of the day, that's all a mother wants for her child."

"Thank you." For the first time since all of this started, I feel like an imposter. This woman thinks I'm madly in love with her son, but that's not the case.

That'll never be the case.

Of course, I care about him, and I like him very much. He makes me laugh, he makes me feel safe. What he does to me in bed should be illegal.

But love?

I'm just not capable of that.

I want to confess it all to her, but before I can say anything, Willa asks, "Your Majesty, if you don't mind me asking, how old were you when you married? I'm afraid I don't know my history very well."

"Oh, that's fine. And, if I'm honest, refreshing." She sits on the sofa, and most of the girls sit or stand around, listening intently.

How often is it that you get a private moment with a queen?

"I was just twenty-two when we married," she begins.

Jenna slides next to me in the kitchen, and as the queen holds court over my tribe, she whispers, "Have you heard from your mom?"

I shake my head. "No. She's not speaking to me. She sent an email and said she wants nothing at all to do with any of this."

"Ouch."

"It's a relief. I don't want her here."

Jenna simply nods and wraps her arm around my lower back. How could I have ever thought that she wasn't right for my brother? For our family?

I don't know what I'd do without this group of women in my life.

"And as for my dad," I continue quietly, "who gives a shit?"

"I'd better be going," the queen says twenty minutes and two glasses of bubbly later. "I know you girls want to talk freely, and you can't do that with me here. I just couldn't resist poking my head in to say hello."

"I'm so glad you did." I offer her a kiss on the

cheek and hope I didn't just break protocol. "Thank you."

"Oh, it's my pleasure. I'll see you tomorrow."

She nods and leaves, and we all stare at each other for a moment.

"That's the Queen of England," Hannah says. "Holy shit."

Ellie and Catherine laugh at us and then clink their glasses to ours.

"Okay, I want to know what it's like to screw royalty," Grace says. "No offense, ladies."

"None taken," Catherine says with a loud laugh. "Oh, it's refreshing to be able to chat like this."

"I don't know what it's like," Ellie says and pouts her lips. "Unless I get to shag a prince from another country, which is unlikely."

"Someone must know what it's like to have sex with *you*," I point out, but Ellie's face reddens, and she just sips her bubbly. "Wait. You're a *virgin*?"

"Do you know how hard it is to meet people when you're a princess?" she asks. "People who aren't boring arses. And can I just say, yes, I'm dating someone, but he's a total wanker, and I'm only seeing him because my father thinks he'd make a suitable husband."

"You haven't had sex with him?" Catherine asks in surprise. "You've been dating for more than a year."

"No. He's too handsy. And when he kisses me, he drools too much. I can only imagine how absolutely dreadful actually shagging him would be."

"Ew," Hannah says with a cringe. "Do you mind if I ask how old you are?"

"Twenty-four," Ellie says with a mournful sigh. "I'm going to be the oldest virgin on Earth soon."

"I doubt that," Jenna says. "And you definitely shouldn't have sex with anyone until he makes you so crazy you can't see straight."

"Don't lose your virginity to a drooling bore," Fallon agrees. "But really, though, what is it like to have sex with a prince?"

All eyes fly to Catherine and me. "You go first," she says, sitting back with her champagne. "I'm comparing notes."

"Who said I've slept with him?"

"Oh, please." Willa rolls her eyes. "Just spill it already."

"I mean, it's nice."

"Nice?" Grace frowns. "You can have *nice* with anyone."

"Not Alistair," Ellie says.

"Okay, it's the best I've ever had," I admit in a rush and can't hold back the big, goofy smile that spreads across my face. "Like, it's *so good*, you guys. Fallon, remember when you asked me if I liked it when guys made sweet, slow love to me?"

She nods, her eyes intent on my face.

"Well, no one ever has before. I mean, it's not like they were jerks or anything, but slow, sweet sex hasn't been my experience."

"She's going to make me cry," Hannah says. "I've had too much champagne."

"And we have all kinds of sex," I continue, clearly also having too much alcohol in my system. "Hot sex, sweet sex. Up against the wall and lazy in bed sex."

At least the queen isn't here for this part.

"So, yeah, it's fun. What about you, Catherine?"

She blinks at me, sipping from her glass. "I can't follow that."

"Yes, you can," everyone replies in unison.

"Freddie and I have been married for ten years," she says.

"That doesn't mean you can't have amazing sex," Fallon points out.

"Well, to be honest, in the beginning it was frequent and fun. But then children came along, and now we're lucky to make love twice a month."

"Whoa," Jenna says, shaking her head. "Girl, that's gotta change."

"He's quite proper," Catherine adds. "But, really, I think we just don't make time."

"Make time," Grace says kindly. "You need that time together, especially since you had the children."

"I think I'll rock his bloody world tonight," Catherine proclaims, her glass in the air.

"Yes, get it, girl," Willa says, clinking her glass to Catherine's. "We so needed this tonight. I'm glad we did it."

"Me, too," I say. "We have the bridal shower tomorrow."

There's a knock on the door again, but before I can answer it, Sebastian walks in with all of the other guys.

"It's like watching a hot guy parade," I mumble, but clearly loud enough for everyone to hear because the guys all break out in grins.

"You're here!" Fallon yells and launches herself into Noah's arms. "I haven't seen you in years."

"Or hours." He kisses her lips. "You're drunk."

"We're all drunk," I inform them. "I'm sorry, I know it's not very dignified to get wasted, but it's my bachelorette party."

"You're in your home," Sebastian reminds me and pulls me in for a hot kiss. "You're safe and enjoying time with your friends. There's nothing wrong with that."

"Your mom came in here and drank with us."

He steps back and stares down at me, then looks over at Frederick, who also looks shocked.

"She did," Ellie confirms. "I was gobsmacked too, but she had a good time. She wasn't here long."

"I never thought I'd see the day," Frederick mumbles, then pulls his wife to her feet. "Shall we, love?"

"Oh, yes. I have some sexy things to do to you."

He blinks in surprise again, then turns to me. "You're welcome in the palace anytime, Nina."

We laugh as they leave, and one by one, each couple follows them.

"No one came to gather me," Ellie complains with a pout.

"We can call Alistair," Fallon offers, but Ellie cringes.

"No, thanks."

They shut the door behind them, and Sebastian pulls me into the bedroom.

"The champagne went to my head," I confess and smile at him. "You're so damn pretty. Like, how is it possible that you're so pretty?"

"It really *has* gone to your head, love." He kisses my forehead and helps me out of my clothes.

"Let's get you into bed."

"Oh, yeah." I reach for his cock, but as my hand closes around it, I'm suddenly intensely nauseous.

Dizzy.

Sweaty.

"Oh, God." I stumble my way to the bathroom and manage to throw up in the toilet. It's a complete miracle.

"Oh, Nina." I feel him playing with my hair, but I don't have time to thank him before the next wave hits me.

"Gonna die."

"I won't permit that," he murmurs. Water runs in the sink, and then he presses a cold cloth to my neck and rubs circles on my back. If I weren't puking my guts out, it would feel heavenly.

It feels like I've been kneeling on the floor for hours when I finally finish dry heaving, and Sebastian picks me up and carries me to the bed.

"I'll be right back." He rushes into the bathroom. Moments later, he's back with a fresh cloth.

He rubs it over my lips, then refolds it and presses it to my forehead.

"Just sleep, darling. Get some rest. It'll help."

My eyes are heavy. I intended to rock his world, but I failed miserably with my incredibly not sexy puke show.

Ugh.

"You should have let me die last night."

My arm is draped over my eyes. Sebastian hasn't even opened the drapes yet, but the little light coming in is already too much. I feel like shit.

I didn't think I drank that much.

But now that I think about it, my glass was always full.

I rub my hand through my hair and pause when I discover that it's braided.

"How did my hair get braided?"

"Well, I could either hold your hair or rub your back. This was much more efficient."

I open one eye and stare at him. He's resting his head on one hand, his elbow braced on the bed. He's naked, but the sheet is wrapped around his waist. I can only see his very tanned, very *toned* torso.

My God, he's hot.

"Thank you."

"Do you have an awful headache?"

I nod and close my eyes again.

"I'll be back."

Do not fall in love with this man, Nina. Love

is off the table. I have to keep reminding myself of that because he's just so *good.* Kind and sweet. Funny. Caring.

He freaking *braided* my hair!

But that's also something a friend would do. It doesn't mean anything. He was being nice, because that's just who he is.

"Here, take this, love."

And just like that, everything in me goes very still. Not the headache, but everything else.

I sit up, take the pills he offers, and swallow them down with water. Then, I stand from the bed, ignoring the sledgehammer pounding behind my eyes.

"What did you call me?"

We're facing each other, completely naked. We should be having wild, crazy sex.

But I need to make sure I heard him wrong.

"You heard me." He braces his hands on his naked hips and frowns at me.

"We promised *no* love," I reply carefully. "No *L* word. You know that's not part of the deal."

He shakes his head and turns away to get dressed. He's not speaking to me, but his actions are quick, clearly signaling that he's angry.

"Why are you mad?" I demand as he ties his shoes. "You *know* how I feel, Sebastian."

I pull his robe around me so I'm not standing there naked as the day I was born.

"Remind me not to be nice to you the next time you've been drinking." He grips my shoulders to move me out of his way and stomps through the apartment to the front door. "Because you turn into a raging bitch."

And with that, he walks out, slamming the door behind him.

I sigh, rub my forehead, and immediately regret everything I just said. He's right, I was acting like a bitch.

I warned him that I could be one.

But he didn't deserve that.

I need to apologize.

I hurry to the door, not giving two shits that I'm only dressed in a robe and last night's makeup. I see Sebastian at the end of the hallway.

"Sebastian!"

But he doesn't turn around.

Nick, along with two other men I don't know, are in the hall and look my way. Nick frowns.

"Miss—"

"I have this handled," Mary says as she comes up behind me. "Come along, Miss Nina, we have plenty to do to get ready for today."

She pulls me into the apartment and shuts the door firmly, then turns to me with a clenched jaw and her hands folded at her waist.

"What were you thinking?" she hisses.

"Sebastian and I had a fight. I needed to apologize."

"Not like that." She shakes her head. "You *never* make it look like he left a room because you had a row and he's mad at you. You discuss things privately. Even though every royal employee signs a non-disclosure agreement, people talk. You just fueled the fire of a scandal, dear, and you of all people should know better."

I swallow hard, feeling the blood drain from my face.

"Oh, God."

I run to the bathroom to be sick again, but it has nothing to do with champagne, and everything to do with how I just left things with Sebastian.

"There's no time for that," Mary says. "You have a bridal shower to get ready for. Now, pull it together, and set it aside until tonight when you and His Royal Highness can make it right."

"It's not that easy."

"Yes. It is. You're a member of this household now, and I'm telling you what's expected of you. Now stop this nonsense and get ready for your party."

I brush my teeth and then shuffle to my dressing room.

For the first time since I met her, I don't like Mary all that much.

Even though she's absolutely right.

CHAPTER 9

"LADY CAMILLA SPEARS."

Camilla nods and smiles, but the expression is as fake as her eyelashes. Just like every other smile sent my way by the dozens of British women I don't know who have been invited to my shower today.

"Hello," I say and then smile at the young woman in charge of making introductions, whose name I don't remember. "I'm going to get some punch."

I slip away, walking to the table set with punch and finger foods. I don't want to see alcohol ever again.

As I sip my drink, I can hear every word being spoken at the table next to me.

"Goodness, the palace is being overrun by Americans."

"It's a pity," someone replies. I don't know any of their names, but I've been introduced to all of them. It's been two hours of faces and names. Fake smiles and lots of side-eye.

In fact, the amount of side-eye being flung around this party is legendary.

I move away, enjoying my moment alone with a refreshing drink, when I hear someone else say, "I give it a year."

My feet stop moving.

"Are you kidding? It won't last three months. She's a commoner from the States. She may be related to Christian Wolfe, but she's a *nobody.*"

They see me. I don't move.

"Please," someone else replies. "I'll have Sebastian back in my bed before it's time for him to walk down the aisle."

I wonder if it would be frowned upon to pull the girl's weave out of her head.

I glance around and find Nick watching me, the way he always does. He narrows his eyes as if he can read my thoughts.

"You said that about Frederick, too," another woman says. "And he seems pretty happy to me. I don't believe he's come knocking at your door even once."

I smirk and keep moving.

The women in Hollywood can be ruthless, but it seems these *noble* women are just plain savage.

The mean-girl syndrome spans the globe.

Good to know.

"You don't look okay," Fallon says when she finds me. She looks fantastic in a green dress that fits her like a glove and falls just past her knees. Her dark hair is down, framing her pretty face. Why doesn't *she* look hungover? "And the energy in this place is *not* friendly."

"I sense the same."

"Come with me." She takes my hand and drags me to the *Montana* table as I've come to think of it. All of my girls are here, enjoying each other.

"We saw you looking longingly over here when you were being drilled with introductions," Jenna says with a sympathetic smile. "We would have rescued you earlier, but you looked busy."

"I literally know eight people at this party, and there are at least three hundred guests."

I sit next to Willa and do my best not to lean my head on her shoulder.

That wouldn't be dignified.

"If one more person gives me a fake smile followed by a sneer, I might just throw my punch in their face."

"That's frowned upon," Ellie says as she walks up next to me. "But I'd pay to see it."

"Sorry, I shouldn't have said that so loud. I'm trying to remember my manners."

"But some of these women make it hard," Ellie says, shaking her head. "Their evil stares could start wars. In the past, they may have."

"Some have made a point of speaking loudly enough for me to hear, saying they've slept with Sebastian and that he'll be back in their bed before we say, '*I do.*'"

"Who?" Ellie's eyes narrow, and we all look around the room.

"Over there," I say, nodding toward the brunette with the big boobs. "Red dress, implants."

"Well, they probably did sleep together at some point," Ellie says with a sigh. "She's wanted to snag a royal since the day she was born. Hasn't worked, though."

"Ew," Grace says, wrinkling her nose. "I don't like her all the way from here."

"Because you're my people," I say, leaning over to squeeze her hand. "And I appreciate you."

"I think most of these people are here because they're nosy," Willa says with a shrug and bites into a finger sandwich. "They want to see who snagged

Prince Sebastian."

"Completely," Fallon agrees. "They're jealous."

"A few are family and genuinely happy for him," Ellie says. "But, yeah, ninety percent of them are jealous and nosy. They're here to see and be seen. It's all part of being nobility or gentry in this country."

She shrugs and then waves at someone trying to get her attention.

"Sorry, I have to go mingle. I'll be back."

She hurries off, and I sigh.

"I should be mingling, too. But, man, I'm tired. Why don't any of you look hungover?"

"Makeup," Willa says. "Lots of it. Oh, and we all did yoga with Fallon this morning."

"No fair. *I* want to do yoga. It's been *weeks.* Can we please do yoga in the courtyard outside of our apartment the morning of the wedding?"

"Hell, yes," Fallon says with a grin.

"How long does this shindig go?" Jenna asks. "And where are the presents?"

"They've been discreetly tucked away," I reply.

"I think it's wrapping up." Grace glances around. "People are getting antsy and leaving."

"That means I'd better go stand by the exit and

thank them for coming." I stand. "Pray for me."

I didn't think I'd make it through. Is this what it'll be like to be a part of this family? Because spending time with people who only look down their noses at me with disdain isn't my idea of a good time.

Just as I reach the apartment and step out of my shoes, Sebastian walks through the door.

His eyes hold mine as he shuts the door behind him and then props his hands on his hips.

"I owe you the biggest apology in the history of the world," I begin. Everything in me sags in relief when his lips twitch with humor. "This isn't funny."

"You're right. Carry on."

"I shouldn't have snapped at you this morning. You were nothing but amazing last night, and again after I woke up. You didn't deserve that."

"I agree."

"I'm *so* sorry. It's just that the *L* word makes me nervous, even though I know you weren't actually saying that you love me. It's just a word, and I'm stupid for overreacting."

"Also agreed."

I glare at him. "You're not making this easy."

He sighs and tugs off his tie, then walks to me and pulls me against him, wrapping his arms tightly around me.

"I need to apologize, as well," he says, surprising me. "I shouldn't have called you a raging bitch. If anyone else were to use those words directed at you, I'd want to tear them apart with my bare hands. I will never speak to you that way again."

"I mean, you weren't wrong."

"Yes." He kisses my head. "I was."

"I hate that I had to wait all damn day to apologize. I tried to run after you this morning, and about gave Mary a heart attack in the process."

"I can only imagine." He kisses my head. "There's gossip moving through the palace that there's trouble in paradise."

"Oh, God. I'm sorry."

"It's okay. We were bound to hit a rough patch, Nina. Things have been going pretty smoothly, all things considered."

He pulls back and tugs me next to him on the couch.

"But we do need to talk about this because you will *not* dictate to me what I am and am not allowed to feel. I've lived my whole life being told how to manage my emotions, and I won't allow my wife to do it."

I frown. "But we discussed—"

"I don't give a bloody damn what we discussed. You told me what *you* would feel, and I said that I understood. I never said I'd feel the same. Not to mention, *love* is a term of endearment."

"I know."

"You have to stop being so damn prickly about things, Nina. Expecting everyone to fall in line with your expectations is not realistic or healthy."

"Are you a psychiatrist now?"

"Just call me Dr. Sebastian."

I can't help but chuckle. "I don't like it."

"You don't have to."

"Are you saying you're in love with me?"

Don't panic.

"No. I'm saying there may be times I use a term of endearment, and you need to stop overreacting to it."

I nod. "Okay."

"We have to be at dinner in an hour."

"I know."

His eyes narrow on my face. "What's wrong? Didn't you enjoy your party today?"

"No, actually, I didn't. Women are just plain horrible. Especially jealous women. And can I just say that nine out of ten of the girls there would rather have me beheaded than see me marry you? One, in particular, was pretty pouty about not having sex with you anymore."

He swallows hard. "Well, that's…disturbing."

"It was horrible. The only saving grace was having my friends there."

"Does it help to know I have no interest in having sex with any of those women?"

"Not really. I mean, we're entering an *arrangement.* Who's to say you won't decide to sleep with them later?"

He doesn't answer. Well, not with words. Instead, he growls and lifts me off the couch, then stomps into the bedroom and drops me right in the middle of the bed.

He crawls over me, dragging his nose up the material of my dress covering my torso as he moves. With his face buried against my neck, he slips a hand between my thighs and pushes under the elastic of my panties to brush his fingertip over my nether lips.

"You," he whispers. "You're the only one I'm interested in touching like this. Jesus, after the past month, you'd think it would be clear that I'm completely enamored with you. But if you need reminding, I'm happy to do so."

He pushes two fingers inside me, and my back arches in wanton invitation.

"You make me crazy," he growls, watching my face as he drives me insane with just his fingers. I'm lying here, completely clothed, and ready to come any second.

"Same," I manage to moan.

He fumbles with his pants, unleashes his cock, and replaces his fingers with one long, fluid thrust.

"Bloody hell." He traps my hands above my head as he rides me hard and fast. "It's just you, Nina. I'll remind you as often as you like."

I can't speak. All I can do is watch as, after three powerful thrusts, he clenches his jaw and loses control, falling into his orgasm.

He presses on my clit with his thumb, and I follow him over.

I'm fucking exhausted.

It's been the longest day of my life. From my fight with Sebastian this morning, to the horrible party with strangers, and the late dinner with the entire royal family, I'm ready to sleep for about a week.

"We need to meet with Charles and Nick," Sebastian says as we walk to our apartment. We're walking slowly, our fingers tangled, my head resting on his hard biceps.

I've discovered I have a thing for Sebastian's arms.

"At this time of night?"

He squeezes my hand.

"We're running out of time between now and the wedding," he reminds me. "They have some things to go over with us, and this is the only free moment in both of our schedules."

"Okay." I yawn. "I'll do my best to stay awake."

Charles and Nick are waiting for us at the door of the apartment when we arrive. They both offer a head nod as we approach.

"Your Royal Highness," Charles says. "Thank you for meeting with us at this late hour."

"It's quite all right, Charles. Please, come in."

They usher me in first, and then we all sit at the dining table.

"Am I correct to assume that you'll want to have a home in Montana?" Charles begins.

"I *have* a home in Montana," I remind him. "You've been there, remember?"

"Of course. Let me begin again. Your current home in Cunningham Falls is lovely, but it's a security nightmare."

I narrow my eyes. Partly out of irritation, and partly because I'm about to fall asleep.

"There is no fence, no way to keep it safe from people. Our men who remain there have been reporting back to me, and it would be impossible for His Highness to live there for any length of time."

"What do you suggest?" Sebastian asks.

"That leads me back to my original question. Am I right to assume that you'll want a home in Montana?"

"Of course," I reply immediately. "I have family there, and I love it."

"I do, too." Sebastian takes my hand in his and gives it a squeeze.

"I've taken the liberty of printing out several homes that are currently for sale in the area that would be better suited to the kind of security you'll need."

He pushes several pieces of paper our way and folds his hands on the table as he waits for us to look them over.

"This one's out," I say immediately, pushing one of the houses to the side. "I want to be on the lake."

"That's an issue," Nick says, speaking for the first time. "It's too easy to access the house from the water."

"I don't care." I stare him down. "I *love* living on the lake. If you're going to insist I sell my house, the one I paid for by myself and love, then I'm not going to bend on this."

"Agreed." Sebastian pages through the papers and pulls out anything not on the lake, setting them aside. "So, when we take those out of the pile, we're left with three properties."

He spreads them out, side by side for us to look over.

"These homes are huge and millions of dollars." I frown up at my fiancé. "My house wasn't cheap, but there are only two of us, Sebastian. Why would we need this much space?"

"We'll have staff and security," he reminds me. "And my family will certainly want to visit."

Of course, they would. And I'd love having Ellie and Catherine, along with the rest of the family there. I know they'll adore Montana. But the cost seems crazy, even to me.

And my brother owns more property than any one person should.

Well, until I met Sebastian, of course.

"We don't necessarily *have* to buy a house there," I say, biting my lip. "It seems silly to spend that much money on a place we aren't at very often."

Sebastian's ice-blue eyes turn down to me.

"Montana is your home, and we'll have a place

there. Please look at these and tell me which is your favorite."

I lean in again. The house in the middle catches my eye.

"Hey, that's Max's house."

"Max Hull?" Sebastian asks with surprise.

"Yes. He and Willa built a new house right after they got married. I knew he'd be putting this one on the market, I just didn't realize he was doing it so soon. It's a *really* nice place, with a movie theater, and even a guesthouse. The boat slip is ridiculous."

I yawn again. As much as I'm invested in this conversation, I'm just out of gas.

"I think Miss Nina is dead on her feet," Charles says kindly. "Perhaps she should go to bed."

"Good idea," I agree with an apologetic smile. "Sorry, guys. It was a heck of a day."

"I'll walk you back," Sebastian says and then turns to Charles. "I'll return in a moment."

He escorts me to the bedroom and helps me into a black tank and yoga shorts, then tucks me into bed.

"I don't think anyone's done this for me since I was a toddler."

He smiles and kisses my forehead. "I won't be long, darling. Go to sleep."

"Sebastian, it's really not necessary to spend

that much money on a house for me."

He frowns down at me and brushes a lock of hair off my cheek. "Nina, the money is insignificant. I'll also enjoy having a home there."

"I don't want to sell my house," I admit in a whisper. I'm filled with guilt that he'll spend the money, and because I *don't* want to sell my little house. I worked hard for it. "I just love it so much."

"You don't have to," he says, sitting next to my hip on the bed. "Darling, we have many options when it comes to your house. We can use it as a guest house, or you can even use it as an investment and ask Jenna to manage it for you. Selling isn't the only option here."

And just like that, I feel *so* much better. I nod sleepily.

"You're right."

"Go to sleep, love."

He turns off the sidelight and walks out of the bedroom, shutting the door behind him.

Montana.

I miss it.

And part of me feels guilty for that. The royal family has done nothing but make me feel welcome and at home here, despite the circumstances.

But I long for my boat, and my little piece of the lake in Cunningham Falls.

CHAPTER 10

Sebastian

"HOW IS MISS NINA adjusting?" Charles asks when I return to the table.

"Don't look now, Charles, but it almost sounds like you like her."

He smiles and shifts his shoulders. "She's grown on me. Despite the immense pressure of what she's walked into here, she's learned quickly and maintains not only her sense of humor but a backbone, as well. I'd say that's admirable."

"I would, too." I push my hand through my hair. I know Nina's exhausted, and I'm right there with her. It's been a trying few days of meetings and responsibilities. Today's talk with my father, Frederick, and Callum had me both frustrated and elated.

And I have another meeting with the king tomorrow.

"She's doing well," I reply at last. "At least, given what she shows me. She's knackered, and I'm positive she's overwhelmed. Who wouldn't be? But she's calm, and so far has been more than willing to go with the flow. I'm proud of her."

"You should be," Nick says. Nick's not one to speak up often, so when he does, I pay close attention. "Those women were brutal today. I wanted to take a few of them over my knee several times. If she already held the title, they wouldn't have dared to say half of the things they did. They wanted to hurt her, but Nina kept her chin up and ignored them beautifully."

"I'm surprised they were so free with their words with you standing nearby."

"I'm invisible," he says with a half-grin. "They're used to me. I watch but don't say anything, and then they forget all about me. It's almost as if they think because I don't talk, I must be deaf."

"I'll want a list of those who behaved the worst," I say. "I don't know what I'll do with it, aside from being aware of them."

"I can do that," Nick says with a nod.

"What do you want to do about the Cunningham Falls house?" Charles asks. "Shall I see to her cottage being put on the market?"

"No." I shake my head and pin Charles with a stare. "Do *not* do that. I don't own that house, and she doesn't want to sell. She'll probably use it as an investment property, or we can always use it as a guest home."

"Sir," Charles says with a nod.

"But I am going to speak to Max tomorrow about buying his house. I'll buy it as a wedding gift to Nina."

I ignore the surprised look from Charles. Yes, several million pounds in real estate is an extravagant wedding gift.

But she deserves it.

"We won't be returning to London immediately after our honeymoon," I add to both of their dismay. "We'll holiday and spend a couple of months in Montana."

"Sir, we haven't had a chance to scope out this new house, fit it for cameras and security. And I have to talk to my staff to find men to work over there. Most of my employees have families here. This will take some time."

"I know someone," Nick says. "Liam Cunningham."

Charles' eyes narrow. "Is he available?"

"He just finished a job in Korea," Nick says. "And he's retiring from the military."

"Cunningham, as in *Cunningham Falls*?"

"Exactly," Nick says with a nod. "He has family there. Has talked about moving there for as long as I've known him. I'd trust him implicitly with your safety."

"As would I," Charles says thoughtfully. "He's been in the business for years. He's ruthless."

"He's American," I remind them. "How do you know him?"

"Special-ops operators know each other, regardless of the country we work for," Nick says

"The saying is true," I mutter. "It's a damn small world."

"You have no idea, sir," Nick says. "I'll ring Cunningham in the morning."

"Good. See to it, then." I stand, ending the meeting. "Goodnight, gentlemen."

Once they leave, I don't waste time. I call Max immediately.

"I'm sorry if I woke you."

"I wasn't asleep," he replies. "What's up? Do you need something?"

"Yes. I just discovered that you have a lake house for sale. I want to buy it."

He's quiet for a moment. "Right now?"

"Right bloody now."

"It's yours. I'll make some calls and get it off the market."

"I'll have the money wired in the morning."

"Good doing business with you, Sebastian."

I feel the smile spread over my face. "Likewise, Max."

"I've made a decision," my father says as he escorts us under the palace to where the vault lies, armed guards surrounding us. Once we reach the heavy door that houses just some of the crown jewels, the man responsible for them opens the lock, and it takes three men to open the door. "I'll explain more in a moment."

"I thought the crown jewels were kept at the Tower of London," Nina says with a frown as her eyes bounce over the sparkling gems gleaming under the soft lights of the vault.

"Most of them are," I confirm. "But we have some pieces here that aren't on display. Pieces that are worn more regularly, and even some that are rarely seen."

"Wow," she breathes. Her eyes are wide, taking it all in. She hugs her arms around her waist, clearly afraid to touch anything.

"If you'll step over here," Father says, gesturing to a table in the center of the room draped in black velvet. "You'll see we've set out a selection for you to see."

"I don't understand." Nina's gaze finds mine, and then my father's.

"You'll need jewelry for the wedding," Father replies. His voice is kind, his smile reaching his eyes.

It seems most of the palace has fallen under my fiancée's charms.

"Oh," she says and swallows hard. "You're right."

"I recommend the Cartier Halo Tiara," my mother says from the doorway. "I've seen your dress, and I think it would look just lovely."

She walks into the room and lifts the tiara made of hundreds of diamonds, showing it to Nina, who is clearly already overwhelmed.

And we haven't even gotten to the good stuff yet.

"It's absolutely gorgeous," Nina says with a nod. "You're right, it's perfect."

"That's settled then," Mum says, setting it aside. She and Nina discuss a necklace and matching earrings, and those join the tiara.

"Now, one more piece," Father says. "I said when I first met you that you wouldn't be given a piece of jewelry from the vault until I approved it."

Nina's eyes fly to mine. "I can't take any of this."

"You're right, you can't." Mum pats her shoulder. "But it can be given as a gift. The jewelry you just chose is on loan from the crown for the wedding day. But we'd like for you to choose something to keep from these pieces."

Mum gestures to several rings, a necklace, and a bracelet. If Nina doesn't like any of these, we have others to choose from.

"If you'd like, you can replace your engagement ring," I offer softly, but Nina shakes her head and looks down at her hand.

"I love my ring," she says.

"A wedding band, perhaps?" Mum lifts a band that's encircled in diamonds. It would fit well with Nina's engagement ring. "This one is about a hundred years old and would be lovely on your hand."

Nina tries it on, considering. "It really is beautiful. But I'd almost prefer something simple that I can wear on my right hand."

She reaches for a ring with a large aquamarine set in the center. It's a simple setting, less grand than anything else on the table.

"This is lovely, and I can wear it with almost anything."

"Are you sure, Nina?" Mum asks.

"It's decided," Father says. "You'll have the wedding band *and* Queen Victoria's aquamarine."

Nina swallows hard. "It belonged to Queen Victoria?"

"It was given to her by the King of Spain," Mum explains. "And it looks lovely on you."

"Thank you," Nina says. "Thank you so much."

"Now that we've settled this," Father continues, "I'd like to tell you that I've made a decision regarding both of your titles."

I stiffen, ready to be told that he's stripped me of all of my titles.

"You, my son, will be His Royal Highness, Prince Sebastian, Duke of Somerset."

"What?" I stare at him and then my mother as she wipes a tear from the corner of her eye. "But I'm giving up my claim to the throne—"

"You're my son, and as such, you'll retain your titles."

I don't know what to say.

Father turns to Nina. "And you will be Her Royal Highness, Princess Nina, the Duchess of Somerset."

Nina's mouth opens and closes, no sound coming out.

"I'm not British," she says at last, her voice quivering.

"You are now," Mum says with a smile. "And we are pleased to welcome you to the family."

"Thank you." Nina licks her lips. "May I please hug you both?"

Father blinks rapidly, but Mum pulls Nina in for a tight embrace. When she pulls away, Nina hugs Father just as tightly, making him blush.

I don't believe I've ever seen my father blush before.

It's bloody fascinating.

"I don't know what to say, except thank you so much," Nina says. "You've been so kind to me, so welcoming."

"You're part of our family," Mum reminds her. "And family looks after family."

Nina's eyes fill with tears. I know that hasn't always been the case for her, aside from her brother. Nina was never able to depend on her parents. Her own mum has been silent, not willing to participate in the wedding festivities, all because of hurt feelings and pride.

I know that despite her shrugging it off, Nina's disappointed in her mother.

"I hope you know that, no matter what," I say as I tuck a strand of her hair behind her ear, "my family will always protect you. Stand by you."

She nods and brushes away a tear. "I'm grateful. And maybe a little overwhelmed. I've always only had Christian."

"We love him, too," Mum says. "And his sweet Jenna. In fact, all of your friends have been a joy to have here in the palace. They're all welcome here, anytime."

"I'm gr—"

"Grateful," Father finishes for her. "We know." His voice is kind. He's not mocking her. "And we're happy to have you here."

It seems my father has a soft side, after all.

Imagine that.

CHAPTER 11

Nina

I'M BLOWING INTO a paper sack, standing in front of an oscillating fan, Julia Roberts-style from *Runaway Bride*.

I'm positive I look ridiculous.

I don't care.

"Do you still think you're going to hyperventilate?" Jenna asks, watching me carefully. She and Ellie have been hovering as Mary and the representative from Givenchy, the designer of my dress, make the final tweaks to the gown.

"I might pass out."

"A princess doesn't faint," Mary says sternly.

"I'm not a princess yet." Jenna holds my gaze, keeping my attention on her. She's so pretty in her pink dress with its matching jacket and hat. "You look really nice in pink."

"It's my signature collah," she says with a wink.

"I love *Steel Magnolias*," I whisper. "Good grief, I'm sweating."

"Do *not* sweat in my dress," the designer says with a pointed stare. "We don't want sweat stains under your arms in your wedding portrait."

"No pressure." I take a deep breath. "It would have been better if I could have seen Sebastian this morning. I wouldn't be so nervous."

"It's bad luck to see the groom on your wedding day," Ellie reminds me as she takes the paper bag out of my hand and replaces it with a glass of water. "Drink this. No more blowing in that thing. You're ruining your makeup."

"You're bossy," I accuse her. Ellie laughs.

"I'm the youngest. Of course, I am."

"She's ready for the veil," Mary says, and Jenna retrieves it from the hanger, then passes it to Mary.

"It's the best part," Ellie says as I bend at the knees so Mary can attach the lace to my tidy up-do.

"There now," Mary says as she steps back, and everyone stares at me. Ellie starts to cry. Jenna grins.

"I've never seen a more beautiful princess."

I turn at the voice, relieved to see my brother.

"You're biased."

"Not even a little bit." He kisses my cheek before turning to his wife. "You and Ellie should get over to the church. I've got it from here."

"Okay." Jenna hugs me carefully, Ellie does the same, and then they're off. Mary and the dress designer help me gather my skirts to walk out to the car.

"I'd like to talk to my sister for a moment."

"We'll be right outside." Both women leave.

"Have you heard from Mom?" he asks, his blue eyes clouding with concern.

"No." I shrug and skim my hands down my skirt. "She swore she wouldn't be a part of this, and you know Mom is too proud to go back on that kind of promise."

"It's her loss, Nina," he says. "If she's willing to let her own pride stand in the way of watching her only daughter get married, she doesn't deserve to be here. But I'm sorry that she's hurt you."

"It's what she does." I shrug again. "Now, let's not talk about her."

"Okay, I have other sweet things to say."

"Don't get mushy on me now."

Christian smiles and looks me up and down as if he can't believe his eyes.

"I never imagined this is where we'd end up,"

he says after a moment. "Me with the woman of my dreams, and you, a princess."

"I mean, I've always *been* a princess."

He laughs. "You know what I mean. It's your wedding day. Let me be mushy for five damn minutes."

I mimic buttoning my lip and wait for him to gather his thoughts.

"I know you don't think you deserve to be loved," he begins. "That being in love is risky and doesn't last. But I've seen the way Sebastian looks at you. Royal or not, he's a man who cares for you. And that makes me happy. I know you have your reasons for this marriage. I respect that. But seeing you together these past couple of weeks has eased my mind a lot. You care for each other, and you're good together."

"I think so, too."

"If you ever need *anything*, I'm only a phone call away. And I may not be royalty, but I'm just as rich, and I can get to you no matter what."

"I know, and I love you, too."

He smiles that million-dollar smile that's been plastered on countless magazines and offers me his arm.

"Just to warn you," he says, "there are literally millions of people in front of the church. This is being televised live across the globe."

"No pressure at all," I repeat. "Jesus, Christian. I'm not the actress in the family. I'm scared shitless."

"Smile. Don't look anyone in the eye until you see Sebastian, then just hold onto him."

I nod as he opens the door, and we're ushered out to the car.

Once we're on our way, my eyes almost bug out of my head.

"You weren't kidding."

People, thousands of them, wave and yell. Hold signs and try to get our attention.

"They like you," Christian says.

"I'm glad," I whisper and wave back, offering smiles. "This is so weird."

We only drive for about ten minutes before we arrive at the chapel. Christian exits the car first and walks around to help me out.

When I step on the concrete and manage to pull all of my dress out with me, I turn and smile at the loud crowd.

"Just wave," Christian says. "And come on, we have to get you married."

I hold onto him for dear life, clinging to his arm as we walk through the doors. The orchestra begins to play the song we agreed on, and I do as Christian recommended.

I don't look anyone in the eyes.

I just smile.

I don't think about the rich and famous watching me. The King of Denmark.

Brad Pitt.

Holy shit, Brad freaking Pitt is here.

I don't even know what I think I'm doing.

But then my eyes find Sebastian, and everything else fades away. His jaw drops in that way every girl wants when he first sees her on their wedding day. And now, all I can think about is getting down the aisle to him.

"Who gives this woman to be wed to this man?"

"I do."

My brother's voice is strong. He passes my hand to Sebastian.

"You're stunning," he whispers. "I'm the luckiest man alive."

And just like that, the nerves are gone.

I'm ready to marry my prince.

CHAPTER 12

Sebastian

"**I**T'S HAPPENING," CALLUM says as he walks into my dressing room, already dressed in his military uniform. He's in red, I'm in a suit, having chosen not to wear my uniform.

Callum is my best man today. It's tradition for it to be a brother, and Frederick will be sitting next to Father as the new next in line to the throne.

Harrison is checking items on his clipboard.

"I haven't seen much of you since I've been home," I reply to my brother.

"I've been in Australia for a few weeks," he says with a shrug. "You know how it is, we all live here, and yet…we don't."

"I live here full time and never see any of you," Harrison adds.

"I know. I just miss seeing you. Both of you."

"Perhaps I'll come to Montana to spend time with you there," Callum says thoughtfully. "Away from the madness of London and our responsibilities here."

"It's quiet in Montana," I agree. "You'd like it."

He smiles. "I could use some quiet. How's Nina?"

"Beautiful."

His smile grows. "I know that part."

"She's surprised me. I thought it would be more challenging for her to learn and fit in, but it's like she was born for this."

"We all like her, even Father, and that's saying something."

"I know." I finish buttoning my jacket and take one more look in the mirror.

"Are you nervous?" Harrison asks.

"No." I turn to both of them. "I thought I would be, but I'm not. I just feel peace about it."

"Then she's the right one," Callum says.

Two months ago, I would have laughed. I chose her because her resume was appropriate for what I needed.

And now? Well, it's become much more than that.

"Are you ready for this spectacle?" Callum smiles at me in the mirror. "Charles told me just a few moments ago that more than a million citizens and a million more from other countries have come to the city to get a glimpse of Prince Sebastian marrying the pretty American."

"Let's not forget the camera crews," Harrison adds. "We'll be broadcast live in dozens of countries."

Callum nods. "Charles and the other men will be discreet. It's not good PR to see us flanked by security as we walk down to the church."

"It's all a show," I murmur. "But it's been good for the local economy."

Callum laughs. "True. Not to mention, the country has always loved their Prince Sebastian."

"They love all of us. And they'll love me less when we confirm the media rumors tomorrow that I won't be their king."

"It'll work out, brother." Callum claps my shoulder. "Let's go get you married off, shall we?"

"Let's do it. You have the ring, right?"

He pulls the ring out of his pocket for me to see. "It's safe with me."

I nod, and we walk down the hall and outside, toward the chapel.

The streets are lined with barricades holding

back throngs of people. When we turn the corner, the crowd erupts in fanfare.

Callum and I both smile and wave as Harrison hurries ahead to attend to things in the church. We stop to shake hands. We never sign autographs or take pictures.

It's a rule.

But we're always happy to say hello and shake hands. Give hugs. Kiss babies.

We've been doing this all our lives.

With one last wave at the crowd, we make our way inside the chapel, where all of the other guests are already either seated or mingling. Our parents and siblings will arrive last, just before Nina pulls up in the car with Christian.

Let's be honest, most everyone here is just dying to see what Nina looks like today.

Myself included.

Her dress, her choice in jewelry, everything about her appearance today will be talked about for hundreds of years. Our photo will be in books for generations.

As they say in America, it's a big deal.

Jacob walks over to meet us, pulling us each in for a hug.

"You don't look nervous at all, mate."

"He says he's not," Callum says. "I'll be nervous for both of us."

"No need for that," I say. "It's all under control. Unless you lose that ring. Then I'll thrash you silly in front of a billion viewers worldwide."

I rub my hands together and look around the room. We have roughly eight hundred guests here today in the audience.

Celebrities, including Luke Williams and Will Montgomery. Royals and dignitaries from all over the world.

It's a big deal.

Maybe I *am* nervous, after all.

"Only three hundred are invited to the party tonight," Frederick reminds me as he joins us, shaking our hands. "Just get through the next two hours, and things will calm down a bit."

"You're the shyest of all of us," I say to him. "How did you survive this?"

"Whiskey," he says with a wink. "Let me know if you need any, I have a flask in my pocket."

"Don't be an alcoholic king when it's your turn," Callum says. "It's so cliché."

We're laughing as the occupants of the room stand, and our parents walk up the aisle, stopping when they reach us. My father shakes our hands, and Mum leans in to kiss our cheeks. Jacob returns to his wife and the rest of the group here from

Montana.

Ellie smiles over at me, and I realize that I didn't see her before this. When I frown, she mouths, "*I was with Nina.*"

I love that she's taken such a shine to my bride. That my whole family has, really. This would be much more difficult if they didn't approve of her.

The crowd outside erupts in fanfare, and I turn to Callum.

"Seems she's here," he murmurs. "Are you ready?"

"Hell, yes."

We're standing at the altar now, our hands folded in front of us, waiting with the priest as the doors open.

Music from the royal orchestra fills the sanctuary.

Everyone stands once more.

And there she is.

Her dress is absolutely stunning. Long, lacy sleeves cover her arms, but it falls over her shoulders, exposing them tastefully. Her veil isn't over her face. Instead, it flows behind her as if there's a wind blowing just for her.

She's a damn angel.

My God, I *am* in love with her. Desperately and irrevocably.

Nina's arm is looped through Christian's as he escorts her through the hundreds of people. Her eyes are pinned to mine, a smile frozen on her face.

She's scared to death.

When they reach the front of the church, we all wait as the song finishes, and then the priest begins.

"Who gives this woman to be wed to this man?"

"I do," Christian says, calmly and loudly, then passes her hand to mine.

I can't stop smiling, looking into her gorgeous eyes.

"You're stunning," I whisper to her. "I'm the luckiest man alive."

Her shoulders sag as if in relief.

"Thank you."

Her smile widens, no longer there as a mask but genuine now.

I loop her arm with mine, cover her hand, and we both turn to the priest.

The ceremony is long, as all royal weddings are. But we speak of commitment, responsibility. Humility. Fidelity.

We even speak of love, and she doesn't stutter over the words.

And, finally, after we've exchanged rings and are pronounced husband and wife, we walk back down the aisle and out the doors to meet the crowds beyond.

"Wow," she says with a sigh. "We did it."

"We did it, darling." I pull her to me and kiss her passionately in front of all of the people gathered. They cheer loudly in response.

"Congratulations," I whisper against her lips. "Princess Nina."

CHAPTER 13

Nina

"**W**HERE ARE YOU going on your honeymoon?" Callum asks as he whisks me around the dance floor.

We're several hours into the reception, hosted by the king and queen in the courtyard of the palace. I changed into a sleek, sexy white dress more suited to dancing after the ceremony. And thank goodness for it because I've yet to sit out even one song.

"Aruba," I reply with a grin. "I'm going to be lazy on the beach with all of the iced tea I can handle."

"I've never understood the American fascination with ruining perfectly good tea with ice."

"Well then, you've never had it prepared properly."

"Perhaps that's it," Callum says with a laugh. "By the way, the Queen Victoria ring suits you."

"I still can't believe I'm wearing it," I murmur. "And I can't believe you know what it is."

"We're taught at a young age to recognize the different pieces of jewelry. We're taught a lot of things."

"Seems so."

"I'd like to cut in."

"Enjoy," Callum says, backing away.

"Your Majesty." I curtsy, and then I'm swept up in the king's arms, being led around the floor.

"Princess Nina," he says with a smile. "Ah, you're not used to that yet, I see."

"I don't know if I'll ever be used to it," I admit. "It's rather surreal, isn't it?"

"I wouldn't know. I've carried a title my entire life."

"Of course." He spins me out and then back in again, making me giggle. "You're a wonderful dancer."

"I had lessons as a boy. And my wife quite enjoys dancing, so I've not let myself get rusty."

I can just picture them dancing like this in their home, and it makes me smile.

"You're not as intimidating as I once thought."

"Don't let it get out. We can't risk being attacked by Germany again."

I laugh again, quite charmed by him. "Sebastian resembles you. Not just physically, but in his sense of humor, as well."

He sighs and glances over to where Sebastian is dancing with his mother. "I was always very stern with my eldest child. I was grooming him to be a king, and I thought that meant withholding emotion from him. It's how I was raised. I regret that more than I can tell you."

"He loves you," I murmur. "He admires you. He's been so worried about disappointing you."

"It'll be an adjustment, but it's nothing we can't move past. You're a wonderful young woman, Nina. If I didn't believe that, we wouldn't be dancing right now. There wouldn't have been a wedding at all."

I believe him. Even as headstrong as Sebastian is, I believe that if his father didn't approve of me, he would have found a way to stop the wedding.

"I'm grateful that there was a wedding."

The song ends, and the king leans in to kiss my cheek. "I am, as well. I'd better pass you back to your husband now."

"Are you trying to steal my girl?" Sebastian

asks as he takes my hand and kisses my knuckles.

"Of course, not. I have a girl of my own."

And with that, Sebastian's parents dance away, swaying to the new song being played.

"Your father has a romantic side," I say as Sebastian pulls me to him and sways to the music. "And he loves you very much."

"Everyone is sentimental today," he replies softly. "Weddings do that to us, don't they?"

"I suppose."

"How do you feel, wife?"

"Hmm...my feet hurt."

"You've been dancing quite a lot. With everyone but me."

"Don't be sad. You can dance with me whenever you want."

He grins and leans in to whisper into my ear, "I plan to do more than just dance with you very soon."

"Really? What sort of things do you have in mind?"

"Well, I'll peel this gorgeous dress off your delectable little body, and then—"

"We're heading out," Grace says as she throws her arms around us both. "We're tired, and we have to go back to the baby tomorrow morning. But it was the *best* wedding I've ever been to in my life."

Our sexy talk over for now, Sebastian and I make our rounds through the room, saying good-bye to our guests.

Everyone from Cunningham Falls is headed home tomorrow.

And we are going on our honeymoon.

I can't freaking wait.

"I finally have you all to myself," Sebastian growls as he closes the door of our apartment and follows me into the bedroom.

I kick off my shoes and sigh when I see my first wedding dress hanging beautifully in the bedroom.

"I don't know what I'll do with this."

"It'll most likely be donated to a museum," Sebastian says, reaching for the pins holding my hair in place. He plucks them out one by one. "Don't worry about it, someone will take care of it."

"That's crazy to me. It's all crazy."

I turn and find him unbuttoning his shirt, then sliding it down his arms.

"You look like a normal man to me. You're sexy and handsome. Your smile could stop a heart at a hundred paces."

"Darling, have you been drinking?"

I laugh and step to him, dragging my fingertips over the rigid muscles of his abs.

"Not a drop. I can't stomach it yet." I lean in and kiss him, right over his heart. "I'm just saying, I'm glad you look normal, that you *act* normal with me."

"There's no other way to be."

He reaches behind me, and slowly—so slowly it makes me hold my breath—lowers the zipper on the back of my dress. When the spaghetti straps slide down my arms and the dress pools at my feet, Sebastian's eyes rake up and down my body.

I'm not wearing a bra. There wasn't any way to wear it without it showing through the fabric. I am wearing the tiniest flesh-colored thong, though.

"Jesus, Mary, and Joseph," he mutters, scooping me up, his arm under my ass as he holds me level with his face. "Blimey. We may miss our flight in the morning. I won't be able to let you get out of our bed."

"I'm going to Aruba. Even if I have to go naked."

He grins and carries me to the bathroom, rather than the bed.

"Uh, Your Royal Highness, the bed is that way."

"I want you in the bath," he says simply, nip-ping at my lower lip. "And then the bed."

"I guess I'm dirty."

"Filthy." His grin is naughty as he sets me on my feet. "Let's get you cleaned up."

"Yes, let's do that."

"I didn't realize we had to take care of this before we could catch our flight," I say the next morning over breakfast in the courtyard. "Do you have to be here for it?"

"Absolutely," Sebastian says grimly. "The people will want to hear from me, and it's important that they know I haven't deserted them, that I've just decided to take a different role."

"When do we go?"

He checks the time. "Less than an hour."

He takes a deep breath and blows it out slowly. I've never seen him nervous before. Not even yesterday at the wedding.

"You know, I've wanted this to happen for as long as I can remember. When I was young, I remember watching Frederick and thinking *he would be an excellent king*. I didn't understand why it was up to me to fill those shoes. I love my country, but I don't want to reign as king."

"But now?" I ask, leaning in to listen. I reach

over to take his hand and squeeze it in support.

"It's bittersweet. It's a relief, and maybe a little sad at the same time. Does that make sense?"

"You sound human to me," I reply and cross to him, straddling his lap. I cup his face with my hands and kiss him soundly. "You've got this, babe. I'll be right there with you. Your family supports you. The people will feel that, and it'll all be okay."

His arms tighten around me, and he buries his face in my neck.

"Did you just call me *babe*?"

"It felt like the right moment for a term of endearment. But if I did it wrong, feel free to say so."

"It was quite nice, actually." He kisses my jaw.

Don't look now, Nina, but you might be falling in love with your husband.

That thought scares me more than anything. More than standing in front of all of those people yesterday to exchange vows.

Even more than spiders, and trust me when I say, they scare the bejeezus out of me.

But he needs me today, and I did take vows to be by his side, supporting him through anything that may come our way.

Looks like that starts today.

"I'd better go get dressed."

I move to slip off of his lap, but his hands tighten on my hips, keeping me exactly where I am.

"Not so fast."

He boosts me onto the table, spreads my robe open, and leans over to tug my nipple between his lips.

"I'm quite naked here on the table, Sebastian."

"I see." He kisses down my stomach. "I do enjoy it when you're naked, you know."

"Hmm." I lean back on my elbows as he licks me, just over my clit. "It's convenient for moments like this."

He surprises me by standing, pushing his lounge pants down his hips, and slipping into me. His motions are quick, jerky.

Desperate.

Without words, he makes love to me on the table. It's not comfortable, but it's hotter than hell.

He slides a hand under my ass to tilt my pelvis up just a bit, changing the angle, and I lose my ever-loving mind.

"Oh, my God."

"That's it, love." He bites my neck, then soothes the spot with his tongue. "Go over, Nina. Let go."

I can't resist him. I couldn't if I wanted to.

And I don't.

As I shiver, my pussy contracts around him, and he moans with his own climax.

When my mind clears, I realize that I'm sitting on his breakfast plate.

"I hope you were done eating."

He laughs, breathing hard, and kisses me loudly on the mouth. "Let's get ready for this news conference so we can leave on our honeymoon. What do you say?"

"I say 'hell, yes.'"

He helps me off the table and peels the plate from my backside.

"I might need another shower," I say. "Do I have time for that?"

"If you shower, I shower, and we definitely don't have time for that."

I laugh. "I'm not allowed to shower alone?"

"We're newlyweds." He frowns as if I've just hurt his feelings and bruised his ego. "It's a law that we have sex in every place possible."

"I want to see the law in writing."

He smiles now. "Come on. We'll make time for a shower."

"Oh, no. You're not going to be late because of me."

"They can't start without me." He shrugs and

drags me into the bathroom. "So a shower it is."

"I shouldn't have said anything."

"Come on, dirty lady," he says with a smile. "You can wash my back."

CHAPTER 14

"HIS MAJESTY WILL begin," Sarah, the chief media executive for the palace says to Sebastian as he's fitted for a microphone. "He'll briefly introduce you, then will step back, and you'll take the podium. We'll have your entire family standing behind you, including your new wife so the people can see that you're all together in this decision."

"Understood," Sebastian replies. He hasn't let go of my hand since we walked into the briefing room of the palace, where the rest of the family is already gathered.

Despite no media, the room is still full of security and staff.

The king and queen are talking with Frederick

and Catherine. Ellie and Callum are eating pastries and laughing about something. No one looks sad or upset.

"We didn't invite the press," she continues. "This is a televised announcement, nothing more. So you won't have to take questions."

"There's nothing to question," Callum says as he joins us. "The decision's been made, and that's that. And if I might say, it's the right one."

"Thank you," Sebastian says and sighs when Sarah walks away. "We're interrupting morning tele. That'll piss some people off."

"It wouldn't be a Monday morning if the royal family wasn't pissing someone off," Ellie says with a bright smile. She hugs me close. "How do you feel today?"

"Fantastic, actually. I didn't drink anything yesterday, so no hangover for me. I'm a little tired, but nothing I can't handle. And you?"

"The same." She watches Sebastian with concerned blue eyes. "I'm a little worried about my brother."

"Don't be," Sebastian insists and tugs gently on her ear. "I'm just fine. And in roughly an hour when I'm in the air on the way to Aruba, I'll be even better."

"We're ready," Sarah says, signaling to the cameraman. Nick and Charles stand in the corner, out of the range of the cameras. Harrison is talking with them about something.

I wonder how excited they are to be going to Aruba.

The king takes his place behind the podium with Sebastian standing just to his right and slightly behind him. The rest of us gather behind them, visible to the cameras. We all have pleasant smiles on our faces. Not too bright, but we also don't look mournful.

No one has died.

"And we're live in three, two…" She mouths "*one*" and points at His Majesty.

"Good morning," the king begins. I can't see his handsome face, but his body language is relaxed, and his voice is strong but calm. "We've interrupted your morning to make an announcement. As you know, my eldest son, Prince Sebastian, married Princess Nina yesterday. We are delighted to welcome her to the royal family.

"However, in light of her country of birth, marrying her means that Sebastian is no longer eligible to take his place as king in my absence.

"Sebastian has made the decision to abdicate his position as the next in line for the throne, passing that role on to my second son, Frederick."

The king takes a breath, and I notice Sarah's phone light up, going crazy, I'm sure, with requests for interviews with the royal family.

As a publicist, I can just picture the storm this will create.

"I would like to make it clear," the king continues, "that my son Sebastian is not being thrown out of England. He will retain all of his titles and his place in the royal family.

"And now, I believe my son would like to make a formal statement."

The king turns to Sebastian and shakes his hand, claps his shoulder, and then they exchange places with Sebastian stepping up to the podium.

"Good morning," Sebastian begins. He may be nervous, but he's hard as stone. There's no tremor in his voice. No hesitation. "This decision was not an easy one for me. I would like to assure you that I'm not deserting my country or the people here that I love so dearly. There will be no change in my work, my duties, or my dedication to serving Great Britain to the best of my abilities.

"I'm certain that my brother Frederick will make a wonderful king when it's time for him to do so. I have every confidence that both my father and my brother's reigns will be ones our people will be proud of for many years to come.

"Thank you for all of the love and support you showed to my wife and me yesterday."

Sebastian turns to me and holds out his hand

for mine. I take it and step to him. He smiles at me, then turns back to the camera.

"We had an absolutely splendid day, and part of the reason for that is because we were able to share it with you. As always, the people of our country make me proud. I'm blessed to be your prince, to be a part of the royal family. I am deeply grateful for your support and love."

He nods, Sarah signals for the cameras to stop, and we all sag a little in relief.

"It's done," Sebastian says.

"Do you have to sign papers or anything?" I ask.

"We did that last week," he replies. "We knew we would be busy directly following the wedding."

"Have a great honeymoon," Frederick says, shaking Sebastian's hand. He leans in to kiss my cheek. "Take care of him. He acts like this was no big deal, but it's all show."

"I will," I promise. Catherine, Callum, and El-lie each take their turns saying goodbye. Finally, we're left with just Sebastian's parents.

"I'm proud of you," the king says. From the look on Sebastian's face, I'd say he's surprised by his father's words.

"You are?"

"You're standing up for what you want, for

what you believe in. Your speech was eloquent and kind. You would have made an excellent king, but I understand how you feel. Have a good trip. Keep in touch."

The king hugs Sebastian—*hugs him!*—and then leaves, blinking away emotional tears that he tries to hide.

"Well, that's a first," the queen says as she pulls Sebastian in for a hug. "Your father isn't one for emotional displays."

"I know."

"He loves you." She pats Sebastian's cheek. "As do I. Have a lovely time on your trip."

After all of the goodbyes, Sebastian and I slowly walk back to our apartment, Nick and Charles following a discreet distance behind us.

"If you're not ready to go, we can wait a day or two," I offer.

"I'm ready," he says. "We've been through the stress, now let's go enjoy some relaxation, shall we?"

"Yes." It sounds like heaven. "We shall."

I was wrong. It hasn't been heaven.

It's heaven times a million. It's like if heaven married chocolate and wine and they had spa babies.

It's the best ever.

And as far as wondering how Nick and Charles feel about spending time in Aruba? I wouldn't know. Because in the twelve days we've been here, I haven't seen them once, not since we got off the plane. Whatever they're doing, they're being incredibly discreet, giving Sebastian and me our privacy.

It's like we're normal people. I didn't realize until this trip how badly I needed that.

"You look relaxed, darling."

I'm lying on the net thing that hangs over the water on the deck of our cottage. The whole building is built *over* the water. We can see fish in the bedroom. Fish in the living room. And out here, I can just lie right over the water.

I never want to leave.

"I'm just thinking."

"What are you thinking about?"

"That we're normal."

He cocks a brow as he climbs the ropes to lie next to me. "As opposed to *ab*normal?"

"As opposed to *royal* people," I clarify and close my eyes. On day two, Sebastian had the resort put a big umbrella over this spot so I could lie here as long as I want without being burned to a crisp.

My husband is thoughtful.

"I hate to break it to you, but we *are* royal people."

"Not today," I remind him. "And not since we've been here. I can be lazy. There's no schedule. And I don't have Nick following me like a stalker."

"It's his job to follow you."

I turn my head to look at him and grin when I see his lips twitching.

"It's been nice, just being here with you and no one else."

"It's a relief to hear you'd rather spend time with me rather than with Nick."

I frown. "Why would I want to spend time with Nick?"

"I was convinced you two had a little thing going on when we first arrived at the palace."

His voice is calm and cool, as if we're discussing the weather.

"*What*?" I sit up and stare down at him. "Why in the hell would you think that?"

"He was handsy," he says simply as if that explains everything.

"The man has touched me like three times."

"Exactly. He shouldn't be touching you at all. I

tried to get him reassigned, but Charles didn't have enough men for it."

My mouth gapes. I can feel it. I just don't know what to say.

"You're jealous."

"Oh, I was. Yes. Absolutely."

I lie back down. "Well, you didn't need to be. Nick's handsome and nice and has a good sense of humor—"

Sebastian rolls over me, pinning me to the nets.

"Don't make me kill the man, darling."

I smile. "I wasn't done. He's all of those things, and he'll be a good catch for someone, but I already caught a man. I'm off the market. I thought you heard."

"You're clever, aren't you?" He nips at my lips and settles between my legs.

"This is a net, not a bed. You're squishing me."

"If I were squishing you, you wouldn't be able to talk." He kisses my cheek and down to my neck. "I realized that Nick is also an asset to our security team. I trust that you're safe in his care, and he stopped touching you."

"Pity."

He laughs now, an all-out guffaw that's contagious. I laugh with him, not minding in the least that he really is smushing me down into the net.

"I love how sassy you are." He kisses me, long and slow. "You keep me on my toes."

"It's my job." His hair has grown long over his forehead. I brush it back with my fingertips. "I don't want to leave tomorrow."

"I know."

"I'm not ready for real life yet. I like your family, but I'm not ready for London."

"We're not going to London."

He rolls off me and reaches over to the deck where I have sunscreen set out. He grabs the bottle.

"Roll over, I need to put this on your back."

"Where are we going?"

"I'm not telling you."

I scowl at him before doing as he asks, turning onto my belly.

"You have rope marks all over your skin. You probably shouldn't lay out here for hours at a time."

"I can't resist it. Please tell me where we're going."

"Nope."

"You know, I can call Christian, and he'll send someone out here to beat you up."

"One, I dare him to try. And two, your brother knows where we're going."

"Wait. Everyone knows but me?"

"Yes."

I cradle my face with my arms and sigh in happiness. Sebastian has the *best* hands. I think I need sunscreen year-round. Every day.

Perhaps several times a day.

All over.

"If you tell me, I'll give you the blowjob of your life."

He snickers. "You do that anyway."

"I'll pay you a hundred dollars."

"No."

I sigh. He's not going to budge, and I'm suddenly incredibly sleepy. I just start to drift off, enjoying the way he's rubbing the lotion on my ass when he gives my butt cheek a little slap.

"Get up. We're going swimming."

"I'm napping."

He kisses my cheek, then picks me up and tosses me into the water.

It's not cold, just shocking. When I surface and push my hair out of my face, Sebastian jumps in after me and tugs me to him.

"That was uncalled for."

"I disagree. It was definitely called for. I want to swim in the ocean with my wife once more before we leave paradise."

And just like that, he says sweet things that make me all gooey.

We're in *Montana!*

I'm dancing in the backseat of our car, being driven through town toward my house on the lake.

"This is the best surprise, ever." I lean over and kiss Sebastian's cheek with a loud *smack.* "Like, in the history of the world."

"You're easy to please," he murmurs, smiling as he watches me in my excitement.

Nick's driving the car, and Charles is in the passenger seat. There's a team of security in a car behind us, as well.

"I have no idea where all of you were while we were basking in the Aruba sun, but you all have tanned skin."

"We were nearby," Charles assures me. "We're never far."

I'm excited to see my house. And my friends. Even though I saw them just a couple of weeks ago, I didn't get to spend much time with them.

We were kind of busy.

I'll have to see if we can manage a girls' night out while I'm in town.

"How long are we here for?"

"We don't have a set schedule yet," Sebastian says. "How long would you like to stay?"

"A couple of weeks?"

"We can manage that."

We zoom past the turn-off to my house.

"Oh, Nick, you missed the turn."

But Nick doesn't reply. Sebastian just murmurs, "Be patient, darling."

"Why are you so mysterious?"

He just smiles, and a few miles past my house, we turn down a driveway.

To a house I recognize.

"Oh, we're at Max's house. Are we meeting Jenna and Christian here? Are we having a party?"

"You talk a lot," Sebastian murmurs as he gets out of the car, then circles around to open my door for me. "Welcome home, Your Royal Highness."

I frown. "What?"

"I bought it for you, as a wedding gift." He kisses me lightly. "Welcome home."

"It's been a long journey," Charles says. "Let's get you inside."

"You said you liked this house," Sebastian says as we walk to the ornately carved front door.

"I do. I'm just surprised. You didn't have to do this."

"I wanted to," he says. "And the security has all been taken care of. We have a state-of-the-art tech person who got everything installed. It's ready to go. The guest house has been converted into security headquarters."

I'm led into the living room upstairs where the windows are huge, and the view is incredible.

I missed the lake so much.

"Your Royal Highness," Nick says, catching my attention. "I'd like to introduce you to Liam Cunningham."

A tall man, similar in stature to Nick, offers me a head bow. "Your Royal Highness."

"Liam is the new head of security in Montana," Charles explains. "He'll be in charge of everything here, including the staff. He'll be assigned to Sebastian at all times, just as I am whenever we're in England."

"You're not staying?" I ask him.

"I'm needed in London, but I'll still be with the prince whenever he's in Europe."

"And if I may," Nick says, "I'd like to stay here with you full-time. Liam has plenty on his plate with the prince and running the rest of the team. I'd like to continue as your personal security, no matter where you are."

"Nick. Don't you have family in London?"

"No, ma'am."

I look at Sebastian, who nods. "If it's okay with Nina, it's fine with me."

"Thank you," I say. "Of course, you can stay."

"That's settled then," Liam says. "It's a pleasure to meet you both. As His Royal Highness said, we are fully staffed, and the technology has been installed and is up and running. This house is newer. It was easy to get everything into place. There will be some rules, however."

I raise an eyebrow.

Here we go.

"Of course, you can come and go as you please. I just ask that at least one of us be with you at all times."

I want to reply with something snarky, but Sebastian squeezes my hand.

"We'll discuss the rest as we go," Liam continues. "I'm available 24/7. My apartment is in the guest house."

"Thank you," I say at last and then turn to Sebastian. "Thank you so much for this. You didn't have to go to all this trouble."

"It's no trouble," he says.

"And you bought it furnished."

"Max left everything, yes, and it's fine for now, but I'm sure you'll want to change everything. You can do it room by room, or in one big swoop, it doesn't matter to me."

"This is going to be a lot of work."

"I'm happy to hire someone if you'd rather not—"

"Oh, no. This is all me. I'm so excited to dig into it. Thank you." I leap into his arms and glance around, pleased to see that the men have all discreetly left the room. I kiss Sebastian hard. "This is the best present anyone has ever given me."

"I'm glad." He hugs me tight. "I was worried you'd be angry. That you'd want to choose it yourself."

"I did. I told you I liked it. But, I also don't want to sell my other place, Sebastian. I'm sorry if it sounds like I'm being stubborn."

"It doesn't," he assures me. "Like I said before, you can do whatever you like with it. Perhaps you could ask Jenna if she'd be willing to manage it as a rental for you."

"That's actually a really good idea. There's no way the security team would approve it for family when they visit."

"It would be unlikely," he agrees. "They'd just run into the same security concerns."

I nod, thinking it over. "I guess using it as an income property is a smart way to go for now. I'll call Jenna about it later. Do they know we've arrived?"

"I texted your brother when we landed," he confirms. "They're coming over later for dinner."

"Perfect."

I'm exhausted. When we landed, I wanted nothing more than a nap and maybe a snack. But now, my adrenaline is up, and I want to research all of the different ways I can decorate this gorgeous house.

"I should give you a tour of our new house," I say. "I just realized you've never been here."

"I'm all yours, darling."

"Wait until you see the movie theater. We'll have to have sex in there later. I've always wanted to have sex in a theater, I don't know why."

"You're a bit of an exhibitionist."

"Nah, I just like movies."

CHAPTER 15

Sebastian

"WHEN DO THEY eat? Have coffee? You know, be normal people?" Nina's eyes are narrowed thoughtfully as she blows on her hot coffee and then takes a sip.

"Who?"

"The security guys," she says. We're sitting in Drips & Sips, enjoying some morning coffee and conversation. We haven't even been in town for twenty-four hours, but we've managed to see family and visit her favorite coffee shop already.

She's glowing.

"They eat and drink coffee when they aren't on duty," I reply.

"But they're *always* on duty."

"Not always. There is downtime." I reach over and hold her hand. She's watching the ladies manning the espresso machine, and the people coming and going.

"I'm buying two of these Drips & Sips mugs while we're here to take back to London," she says. "And, am I mistaken, or did I see a *For Sale* sign in the window?"

"I saw it, too," I reply.

"Okay, we have two egg and bacon sandwiches." The server puts our food in front of us and smiles. "What else can I get you?"

"This looks great," Nina says. "But can I ask a question?"

"Sure."

"Why is Anna selling this place?"

"Oh, she wants to move to California to be closer to her grandkids. I'm Aspen. Just let me know if I can get you anything else."

She bustles away, and Nina frowns.

"What's wrong?"

"I don't want someone to come in here, buy the place, and change everything. Drips & Sips is one of the best parts of the town." She takes a bite of her breakfast, then wipes her mouth. "I'm buying it."

"We should discuss this. It's not exactly convenient to own a business."

"Am I not allowed to?"

I frown. "Of course, you're allowed to."

"Well, I can hire a manager, and I won't have to be hands-on. I can just make sure that it stays the way it is now."

She walks to the front of the store, takes a picture of the sign, and then returns to the table.

"I think you just about gave Nick a heart attack just now," I say, watching as Nick's eyes narrow on Nina. "When you made a run for the door, I thought he was going to run after you."

"Oh. Right. Sorry, Nick."

He nods once, and Nina returns to the task at hand.

She dials a number and presses her phone to her ear.

"Hello, is this Jillian King? Are you the realtor for the Drips & Sips listing? Excellent. I'd like to buy it." She deflates. "You're kidding. When?"

"It sold already?"

She nods. "Yes, put me down as a secondary buyer in case the other one falls through. My name is Nina Wolfe."

"Nina Wakefield," I remind her.

"Oh, sorry. I'm Nina Wakefield. I just got married, and I'm still getting used to the name change."

She flashes me an apologetic smile.

I'll remind her exactly who she belongs to when we get home.

"Yes, that Nina Wakefield. Oh, thank you so much. Okay, if it goes back on the market, please let me know. Have a good day."

She hangs up with a deep sigh.

"Well, damn it."

"Did she say who bought it?"

"No, she probably can't do that. She just said it sold this morning. I'm just one day too late. But I'm officially the backup buyer if the sale falls through."

"Maybe the new owner doesn't have any plans to change anything."

"I hope not." She sips her coffee. "What should we do today?"

"I'm with you. What would *you* like to do?"

"Well, I've been here plenty, but never when the weather is good enough to hike in Glacier National Park. Let's do that."

I clear my throat. "You want to go *hiking*."

"Sure. There's no cell service up there. It's a nice day. We can be up and back before dinner."

"You want us to go hike through the woods on

purpose."

She laughs. "Yes. You're a manly man. You ski and do all kinds of things."

"*I* do," I agree. "I'm just shocked that you want to."

"I'm a mysterious woman." She winks at me, shamelessly flirting. "What do you say?"

"Let's go."

Once we're home and the security team has been briefed, Nina and I change into our hiking clothes. She had the rest of her things brought over from the other house last night. She's wearing hiking shorts, a tank top, sunglasses, and a hat.

If I didn't know it was her, I wouldn't recognize her.

"I'll be right behind you," I assure her.

"I'll go put some snacks and water bottles in my backpack."

She hurries out of the bedroom, and I finish getting dressed, then follow the voices to the kitchen.

Nick, Liam, and Nina all stop talking and stare at me.

"What?"

"If I might say," Liam says with a grin, "you can't wear that."

"Why ever not?" I stare down at my khaki

pants, green polo shirt, and loafers. "This is as casual as I have with me."

"I have things you can wear," Liam replies. "I'll be right back."

"We're fine here," Nick says with a nod as Liam hurries to his apartment not even fifty yards away. "I'm sorry, sir, I should have known you didn't have the proper gear with you."

"No, I'm sorry," Nina says. "I should have known. I didn't think about it."

"It's fine. I'll borrow Liam's things today and make sure to have my closet filled with outdoor gear now that I know my wife is an outdoor enthusiast."

"I mean, I could go once or twice a year. It's not like we're training to climb Everest or anything."

"That's a relief," Nick says with a sigh. "Because a casual hike I can do, but Everest is a bit outside my comfort zone."

We're laughing when Liam returns with his clothes. "These are all brand new," he says. "You can keep them if you like."

"I'll pay you for them," I reply with a nod. "Thank you."

"I checked your shoes on my way out, and I have shoes for you, too," Liam says. "They're not new, but they'll work for today."

"I appreciate it. I'll buy some new trainers this week. I'll just go change and be right back."

The best I can tell, we're about three-quarters of our way to the body of water called Avalanche Lake that Nina wanted to hike to. It's just the four of us, and so far, we haven't been recognized once.

Granted, it's not typical for royalty to be in Montana, and I can't imagine most people would expect to see us hiking a trail in Glacier National Park. So, no one is looking for us.

And on top of that, we're all dressed similarly in hiking clothes, with backpacks and hats. Sunglasses.

It's the best disguise I've seen, and it's a fabulous success.

"We should be close," Nina mutters, breathing hard. "And I need to get back into shape. This is ridiculous."

"We're at a higher elevation," Nick reminds her. "It's going to be more challenging until you get used to it."

"*You're* not breathing hard," she says. "In fact, all three of you are breathing like we're just taking a little jaunt in the pasture."

"It's not a competition," I remind her and earn a glare in return. "I saw that through your sunnies, darling."

She just smirks, and then we follow the trail through some bushes. Suddenly, before us, is possibly one of the most beautiful things I've ever seen.

"Wow," Nina says, stopping to pull off her backpack. The lake is before us, snuggled up against a wall of a mountain, with several enormous waterfalls that fall to the lake below.

"This is brilliant," I agree. "Well worth the hike to get here."

"I'm going to dip my toes in," Nina announces. Nick starts to disagree, but I shake my head.

"There's no one here," I say softly. "And we're all nearby."

Liam nods in agreement, and we watch as Nina strips out of her socks and shoes and then wades to her knees in the water.

"It's *cold*," she cries. "So freaking cold."

"It's glacier run-off," Liam says. "It never warms up."

"Fascinating." I follow her lead, taking off my trainers and socks and following her into the water. "Oh, it takes your breath away, doesn't it?"

"Oh, yeah, but it's warming up now. Or I'm getting used to it. Or my legs are going to fall off."

"We can't have that, darling." I lean in to whisper in her ear. "I quite enjoy having these legs on my shoulders while I do wicked things to you."

"I quite enjoy that myself," she says, trying to mimic my accent.

"You sound Australian," I say with a laugh. "Not British."

"I'll get it down eventually." She shrugs a shoulder and climbs onto a boulder that's completely surrounded by shallow water. "Let's sit up here and have lunch. Except our lunch is in my backpack onshore."

"I'll be right back."

I fetch her pack and walk back out to the boulder, climb up, and sit next to her. "Don't look now, but the others are eating, too."

"Seriously?" She whips her head around and grins when she sees Nick and Liam biting into sandwiches. "I packed the food for them and told them they'd better eat it because we're hiking and burning too many calories to be stoic and strong."

"So you threatened the staff. Lovely."

She laughs. "No, I told them to eat. It's silly that they don't eat when they're with us."

"No, it's not." I set my crisps aside and catch her chin in my fingers. "They're *protecting* us. It's not silly because they're doing their job."

"What are they protecting us from?"

"Assassination attempts, over-eager fans, kidnapping." She's stopped chewing and is staring at me with stunned, wide eyes.

"You're kidding."

"I'm not. I get death threats every day, Nina. And someone almost snatched Ellie once when she was very little. Sometimes, it's more innocent than that. Fans want to hug, touch. And if they're particularly brave, they try to grope or kiss."

"Ew."

"Exactly. We have security nearby to control those around us so we can live our lives."

"Well, that's great. But I don't want to be one of those people who ignore them. Pretends like they aren't there. They're human beings, and if they're going to be near me all of the time, I want to be friendly with them."

"You can be friendly, but there is a line. They're not our *mates*. They're employees."

"I understand that." She chews thoughtfully. "Speaking of that, we'll probably need to hire a housekeeper. I've always cleaned my own place, but the new house is way too big for me to keep up with."

"I certainly don't expect you to clean the house." I pop a crisp into my mouth. "Certainly Jenna or Willa must know someone."

"I'll ask them. I spoke to Jenna last night about managing my old house, and she said she'd be glad to. So, I'll have someone go in and give it a good scrubbing, make sure everything is as it should be, and she'll take it over from there."

"I'll go with you to walk through it," I offer. "And I know Liam had one of his men drive the boat down the lake to park it in the boathouse of the new place."

"That boathouse is ridiculous," she says, shaking her head. "I just need one little slip."

"Well, if family visits in the summer, we'll have several boats on hand for them to use. Callum is especially fond of the water."

"Really?"

"Yes, he's in the Royal Navy and is more comfortable on the water than most of us are on land. So, we'll get use out of the boathouse."

"Not to mention, it has its own apartment," she says. "I went down there this morning to look around, and I was surprised to find it. There's more space in that house than we will ever use."

"It's an investment," I remind her. I want to also remind her that we may someday fill it with children, but we're not there yet.

Nina's loosened up a lot with me over the past few weeks. She doesn't tense up when I touch her or use terms of endearment. She's quicker to laugh, and she doesn't watch every move I make with wary eyes.

I've gained her trust.

One day, I hope to earn her love.

But I know that mentioning babies right now isn't the way to do that.

When our lunch is consumed, we stow the garbage in the pack, and I help her off the rock to wade our way back to shore where Liam and Nick are waiting.

"Shall we head back down?" I ask.

"We probably should," Nina says. "But thanks for this. It was a great day."

Nina's been gone for an hour. I'm alone in the house, thanks to the technology Liam spoke about the other day, and security patrolling the perimeter of the building.

I should be catching up on the dozens of emails that have come in since I left London. Or reading. Anything, really.

But instead, I'm sitting here like a sap, missing my wife.

She's been gone for an *hour.*

Nina went to a local florist shop with her friends for a girls' night out. Nick's with them, and I'm sure they're having a smashing time. I was sure I'd take advantage of the time alone to catch up on work.

The most I've managed to do is open my laptop.

I suppose I should have rung Jacob to see if he'd like to have a beer. I still could, in fact.

But just as I pull my mobile from my pocket, it rings, Christian's name on the caller ID.

"Hello?"

"Hi. I'm sorry to interrupt your evening. I'm not sure what to do here."

"What's wrong?"

He's quiet for a moment. "I feel like a dick for not telling Nina first, but I know she's with Jenna and the others having fun, and I didn't want to fuck that up."

"Christian, what's going on?"

"Our mom died today."

I blink, staring out the windows into the dark night. "Oh, Christian, I'm sorry."

"I wasn't close to her," he says. "And neither was Nina really, but she's going to be sad. I just don't know what to do."

"Come over," I reply. "I'll call Nick and have him bring the girls. Then you can tell her."

"That's a good plan. Thank you."

"You're welcome, of course. I'll see you soon."

"Oh, and I should mention," he adds, "my sister can be mean when she's sad. I just want to warn you."

"Duly noted. Drive carefully."

I hang up and let out a long breath. It seems tonight just went into the shitter.

I dial Nick's number.

"Yes, sir."

"I need her home. Both her and Jenna. Right away."

"Yes, sir."

Nick ends the call, and I close the computer and walk into the kitchen to get a pot of tea brewing. It's the best I can do for right now. Until she's here and knows what's happening and can tell me what she needs.

I'm in new territory.

CHAPTER 16

Nina

"CITRUS POPPYSEED CAKE with huckleberry filling, anyone?" Maisey Henderson asks as she swoops into the room, carrying a tray of delicious goodness. Maisey owns Cake Nation, the best bakery in town, and her sister, Brooke, is the owner of Brooke's Blooms.

Their shops are located on Main Street, right next to each other, which is perfect for the parties they host.

Tonight, we're here learning how to make pretty fall flower bouquets while we sample Maisey's *amazing* cakes.

"Yes, please," Jenna says, immediately raising her hand. "I need all the cake."

"Same," Willa says. "The more cake, the better. Also, I need to order a birthday cake for Max. I know it's still a few months out, but you book up fast these days."

"We can do that," Maisey assures her.

"Actually, I think I need a cake for Sebastian," I add in surprise. "You guys, his birthday is coming up. This is our first occasion together, aside from our wedding, of course. What do I do?"

"Well, you order a cake, invite some people over, and have a little party," Fallon says with a smile. "Your new house is perfect for it."

"Is it weird that I'm living in your husband's old house?" I ask Willa.

"Not at all. We have a fabulous *new* house," she says with a smile. "And Fallon's right, that house is awesome for parties. We'll help you plan something."

"I need to invite his family." I reach for my phone and shoot a text off to Ellie, asking her how I should handle this.

> *Me:* Hey, sister-in-law. Sebastian's bday is coming up in a couple weeks. Would you guys like to come to Montana for a party?

I set my phone aside, take a bite of the strawberry cake still on my plate from a bit ago, and concentrate on how to fit the greenery and flowers together without it looking like a whole bunch of weeds.

"This is an art form." I smile across the table at Brooke, who's helping Jenna get her flowers under control. "I feel like I'm all thumbs."

"It just takes some getting used to," Brooke says. She's a beautiful and kind woman.

"Would you like some cake, Nick?" Maisey asks my bodyguard. I glance over in time to see him shake his head *no*.

"Come on, Nick. Eat the cake. I won't tell."

His eyes narrow on mine. "No thank you, ma'am."

"He's hot," Fallon whispers so only I can hear. "I mean, my husband is the hottest man on the planet, but if I were in the market…"

"I know," I whisper back. "And he's really nice. Do we know any single girls?"

"Not really, but I'll keep my eyes open."

"Why are you whispering?" Jenna demands. "Share with the rest of the class."

"Not a chance," I say with a laugh as my phone pings with a return text from Ellie.

> *Ellie:* YES!!! Of course I want to come! Mum and Father probably can't, but I'll see if the

others are available. Will up-
date soon! Miss you. Xo

Me: Why are you awake? Go to
sleep!

Ellie: Then stop texting me!

I laugh and set my phone aside. "Looks like Ellie's definitely coming for Sebastian's party."

"That's awesome," Jenna says. "I really like
her. I liked all of them."

"Me, too." I shove some green leaves into the
vase and frown. It just doesn't look right. "What
does one get a prince for his birthday?"

We all look over at Nick, but he just shakes his
head and actually cracks a smile. "Don't ask me."

"Your accent doesn't sound British," Jenna
says thoughtfully.

"No, ma'am."

"Where are you from, Nick?" Brooke asks. Before he can answer, his phone rings.

"Yes, sir."

His eyes shoot to mine.

"Yes, sir," he says again, ends the call, and
puts the phone into his breast pocket. "Your Royal
Highness, I have instructions to take you and Miss
Jenna back to your house right away."

"What's wrong?"

"I don't have any other information, ma'am."

"I don't know if I'll ever get used to people calling you *Your Royal Highness,*" Fallon says with a grin. "Go ahead and go. Keep us posted."

"I hope everything's okay," Willa adds. "Text us both, okay?"

"Will do."

Jenna and I grab our things, say our goodbyes, and then we're in the car on the way home.

"I wonder what's going on," Jenna murmurs. "Christian isn't responding to my text."

"We'll be home in a minute," I murmur.

I have a bad feeling.

A second security guard, not Liam, meets us at the car, and they escort us inside.

"His Royal Highness and Christian are in the living room, ma'am."

"Thank you." Jenna and I hurry into the room and find our husbands sitting opposite of each other on the couches, each with a somber look on his face. "What's going on?"

"Come here, darling."

I cross to Sebastian and sit next to him. Jenna does the same with my brother, but Christian's eyes are on me.

"Chris, what's going on?"

"I got a call this evening from L.A.," he says and swallows hard. "Mom was found earlier today, Nina. She passed away."

I cover my mouth with my hand, my eyes wide and pinned to my brother.

"How?"

"I don't know yet. That's really all I know."

Sebastian wraps his arm around my shoulders, but I don't lean into him. I feel frozen. I feel sick to my stomach.

"It's my fault."

"I'm sure that's not true," Sebastian says quietly.

"No, it is. It's my fault. She told me she wasn't feeling well, and I blew it off because she was always complaining. I should have listened."

"Nina, we don't know what caused her death," Jenna says strongly. "Honey, don't do that to yourself. We *don't know anything.*"

She sits on the other side of me and hugs me tightly.

I can't look away from Christian.

His lips are pressed into a thin line. His eyes look tortured.

"I'm sorry that I interrupted your fun evening,

but I wanted you to know right away."

"This was the right thing to do," I assure him. "Thank you. I assume we're headed to L.A. soon?"

"Tomorrow morning," he confirms. "I have the plane ready to go."

"I've briefed my men, and they're ready to go when we are," Sebastian says with a nod. He takes my hand, and I squeeze his, hard. It's like he's the only thing grounding me right now.

"Let's plan to meet at the plane at around eight," Christian suggests. "It's a relatively quick flight. That will give us most of the day to make arrangements."

"That works for us," Sebastian says with a nod.

I stand when the others do, out of habit more than anything, and when Christian wraps his arms around me and hugs me close, I begin to cry. It's as if a dam has broken and I can't hold it in anymore.

"I don't know how to feel," I admit.

"I know," he whispers and kisses my forehead. "It's going to be okay, sis. Honest."

I'm sobbing in earnest, harder than I have since I was a small child. I feel him kiss me again, and then he moves me into Sebastian's arms, where I'm cradled and petted. Sebastian murmurs words of encouragement and affection, and it only makes me cry harder.

I don't deserve his kindness.

"Do you need me to stay?" Christian asks softly. I shake my head *no*. I'd honestly rather that he not see me like this. "Okay, then. I'll see you in the morning. But if you need me, just call, sweetheart. I can be here in minutes, okay?"

I nod in agreement, feel both him and Jenna kiss my cheek, and then Sebastian and I are alone.

He carries me into the bedroom and lays me on the bed, then crawls up next to me and pulls me into his arms once again.

"I don't know why I'm crying," I say between hiccups. "It's silly."

"Your mum died, darling," he reminds me. "Of course, you're crying."

"But I don't think I'm crying because I'm sad." It's a whisper. "I'm so ashamed, Sebastian. I don't know what I'm feeling."

"Talk it out." He passes me a tissue. "I'm not going anywhere. Lean on me, love."

Love. God, I'm falling in love with him, and I can't. I'm not supposed to feel this deeply for him.

I'm just a whole mess of feelings.

"Of course, it's horrible that she died," I begin. "And I *am* sad that she's gone. But at the same time, I feel relieved, and *so guilty* that I feel that way."

"Why do you think you feel relieved?"

I don't want to answer him. "I don't know."

"Yes, you do." He tilts up my chin so he can look me in the eyes. "You're safe here, Nina."

"Because now I don't have to worry about her anymore," I blurt in horror. "She was so *hard.* And unkind. And I hated what she did to Christian. But I felt obligated to have some sort of relationship with her, and now I don't have to do that anymore."

I bury my face in his chest and cry some more. For the girl who never had a mother she could depend on and look up to. For Christian, who was so hurt by the woman who gave birth to him.

And for myself, the woman who won't have a relationship with her mother. Mom won't be here if I have children. She didn't even come to my wedding. And the worst part? I didn't want her there because she had a habit of embarrassing me and she wasn't a nice person.

Sebastian doesn't try to tell me that I shouldn't feel this way. He doesn't try to cheer me up. He simply lays with me, rubbing circles on my back and kissing my hair.

I feel loved. Supported. Cared for.

And it scares me. Because it's not forever. Someday soon, it'll be gone.

Don't learn to depend on this, Nina.

We've been in the air for forty minutes. Christian, Jenna, Sebastian, and I are in plush seats, sitting across from each other. Liam and Nick are in the back of the plane, murmuring to each other.

Most likely figuring out security for once we land.

"I just thought of something," I announce. "Where are we going to bury her?"

Jenna frowns and looks at her husband.

"She doesn't have any other family. We're never in California unless you're there for work," I continue. "It doesn't make sense to take her to Montana. She never set foot in the state."

"We'll have her cremated," Christian says softly.

"I know this makes me a raging bitch, but I do *not* want her on my mantel." I shake my head adamantly. "No way. I mean, do *you*? That's just creepy."

"No mantel sitting," Christian agrees with a small smile. "I was thinking we'd spread her ashes in the ocean, in front of her house. That was her favorite place anyway."

I nod slowly. "Yeah. Yeah, that's fine."

I take a deep breath and lean my head on Sebastian's shoulder.

"Did she have a will?" Sebastian asks.

"Not that we know of," Christian answers. "I own her house. I bought it for her about ten years ago after she went bankrupt and was going to have to live on the streets."

Jenna links her fingers with Christian's in support.

"I'm sorry." I feel my eyes filling with tears again. It's a miracle I can even see today, they're so puffy and red from crying on and off most of the night. "I'm so sorry for everything she put you through. And despite stealing from you and wasting *millions*, you still made sure she was taken care of."

"It's easy to do when you can throw money at a problem," he says with a shrug. "You're the one who had to listen to her. To check in on her. What you did was way more difficult."

"I think you were both making the best out of a challenging situation," Jenna says.

"I agree," Sebastian adds. "You were both loyal to her, in your own ways, despite her being hard to deal with."

"We're not perfect," I mutter. "And she reminded me of that often."

"She can't hurt us anymore," Christian reminds

me.

"I think she loved us, in the only way she could."

"I don't," he says. "She chose the way she behaved. Her need for attention and fame in her own right overtook her instincts as a parent, and it cost her the love of both of her children."

"And isn't that a shame?" Sebastian says softly. "Because she lost out on two wonderful people."

I glance up at him and squeeze his hand. "Thank you for that."

"You're welcome. It's going to be a rough couple of days. What do you two need from Jenna and me?"

"Yes," Jenna says, "what can we do?"

"Just be here," Christian says. "The moral support is the most important piece. I honestly don't know what we're walking into. We'll go directly to the coroner's office from the airport. They want us to identify the body."

"*Christian.*" My voice is a squeak. "No one's identified her?"

He swallows hard. "They know it's her because she was found at home, but they need a family member to confirm."

"Who found her?" Jenna asks.

"I've had a home health nurse looking in on her

since her heart attack. She goes twice a week."

I'm staring at my brother, dumbfounded.

"I didn't know that."

He shrugs a shoulder. "I thought it was best to hire someone to look in, make sure she was taking her meds, had groceries, that sort of thing."

"She never mentioned it."

"Of course, she didn't," Christian says with a humorless smile. "She wanted to keep painting herself as the victim, and me the bad guy. I can only imagine the things she's told you about being alone and unable to go places."

That's exactly what she told me.

"It was a lie. Sandra went twice every week, and sometimes more if Mom had appointments or other things she needed."

"I can't believe she didn't say anything." I rub my hand over my eyes. I'm not wearing makeup. I cried it all off, and adding more seemed a waste of time.

"I'm sorry, darling." Sebastian kisses my temple.

"Me, too."

We land in L.A. and are immediately ushered into a limo and driven to the coroner's office, where we enter through a back door.

Liam and Nick were constantly talking into

their phones during the journey from the airport and are all business as they escort us into the building.

"This way, please," the doctor says, gesturing for us to sit in a conference room at the end of a hallway. "I'm Dr. Garcia. I'm very sorry for your loss."

Number one.

There will be hundreds of *sorry for your loss* platitudes coming our way.

I hate that expression.

"Thank you for coming all this way," Dr. Garcia continues. "As you know—"

"We don't know anything," I interrupt. "Can you please tell us how she was found, and what happened?"

"Oh, of course. Your mother was found yesterday afternoon at around two." He frowns and looks at his hands on the table.

"You can be frank with us," Christian says.

"We think she was deceased for about four days before she was found," he says at last.

"How did she die?" I ask.

"Your mother was on blood thinners after her heart attack, correct?"

"Yes."

232 | KRISTEN PROBY

"Her doctor recently changed her medication, but we think she was confused. Rather than switching to the new med, she began taking them *both*. Which was catastrophic for her. It seems she cut herself on something and bled out rapidly. There was no way to save her, even if someone had been with her."

"Oh, my," Jenna says on a sigh.

"So, it was an accident?" Sebastian says.

"Yes, sir," Dr. Garcia replies. "There was no evidence of self-harm, or of anyone else being there. It was an accident."

I stand, pushing the chair out from under me. "I'll identify her now."

"No, Nina, I'll do it," Christian says, but I'm already shaking my head no.

"You haven't been in the same room with her in years."

"I was there when she had the heart attack."

"Briefly. And I'm not saying this to make you feel guilty or to hurt you. I'm not angry at you. I just think it should be me. You don't have to do this. She did enough to you."

Christian stands and takes my hand. "She did enough to both of us. We'll go together."

I blink rapidly, not willing to let the tears fall as Dr. Garcia leads us down the hall to another room that's empty aside from a gurney and a body covered with a sheet.

Sebastian, Jenna, and the others wait in the hallway as we go into the room and stand next to the gurney. Dr. Garcia stands across from us as he grips the sheet.

"We just need a positive identification," he says and then peels back the linens.

I don't know what I expected, but it isn't this.

She looks...*peaceful.* Pale. Her lips are blue. Her eyes are closed, and maybe for the first time in my life, she doesn't look angry.

"It's her," I say.

Christian nods in agreement and then escorts me back to the hallway. Sebastian takes my hand, and we leave out the back door, headed to the limo.

"Let's go home," Christian says. "My house is ready for us."

"I need a nap," Jenna says. "And maybe a swim in the pool."

"What about you, Nina?"

"I need a stiff drink."

"We can do that, too."

CHAPTER 17

"YOU SHOULD EAT something."

I'm sitting across from Sebastian at a small table by the pool at Christian's house. It's early in the morning. The sun has just barely risen.

I didn't sleep much last night. I couldn't get her face out of my mind, so I spent hours tossing back and forth. I even got out of bed for a while and sat out here by the pool, watching the moonlight shimmer on the water.

At least I've stopped crying.

"I'm okay."

He frowns at me over his iPad. I'm not sure what he's been reading.

"You haven't eaten in almost two days."

"Thanks for counting."

His icy blue eyes narrow on me, and I know I'm being horrible. "I'm sorry. I know I haven't eaten, I'm just not hungry."

"We all need to eat," Christian says as he and Jenna join us, carrying trays of fruit and pastries. They each choose a seat, and we nibble in silence, half-heartedly choosing from the platters of food. "Did you sleep at all?"

I shake my head *no*. "You?"

"Not much," he admits and pours himself a cup of coffee. Nick and Liam join us on the veranda, sitting nearby, looking refreshed and ready to go. "We should leave early this morning so there's less press."

"Why would there be press?" I ask and immediately regret the words. "Never mind. I know why."

"Why?" Jenna asks. Jenna's always put-together. *Always.* But even she looks a little worse for wear this morning.

"Because he's Christian Wolfe, and I'm married to him." I point my thumb at Sebastian. "Which means, this is a story. So the press will be camped out, wanting comments."

"If we go early, there's less chance the press

will be around," Christian says.

I turn to Sebastian and reach for his hand. "You don't have to go with us."

I'd rather you not go with us.

This is the part of the trip I've been dreading the most. If I can avoid it by making it sound like I'm protecting him from the press, all the better.

"Of course, I'm going," Sebastian replies. "I'll be wherever you are, you know that."

"Sir," Liam interrupts. "The princess is right. The press could get difficult on this one—"

"Fuck that," Sebastian says, his voice raised in agitation. "I've never questioned the security detail and the importance of you being with us. I follow the rules. But goddamn it, you're asking me to *not* be with my wife when she's going through one of the most difficult times in her life. If you think I'm going to stay here in case the press gets difficult, you don't know me at all. You've been hired to keep us safe. Just do your bloody job, and we'll be fine."

Liam's jaw tics when he nods stiffly. "Sir."

"We'll go after breakfast then," Christian says. He's watching Sebastian with a new light of respect shining in his eyes. "I like you, man."

"At least someone does. I think Liam might want to throat punch me."

"I won't let him do that, sir," Nick says, making us all laugh.

"I don't want you to see this," I admit as we park in front of Mom's house. There's no press parked outside, so we'll call that a win.

"What do you mean?" Sebastian asks.

"It's a shit hole. Not the house itself, but what she's done to the inside of it. It's embarrassing, Sebastian."

He squeezes my hand and kisses my cheek. "Don't worry about it."

Right.

I *am* going to worry about it. He doesn't know what he's talking about.

He hasn't seen it.

But he's about to. And not just him, but Jenna and the security guys, too.

Liam unlocks the door, and each of us has to squeeze through the opening, following a path that leads to the living space where Mom had a chair that faced the big windows that look out onto the surf.

"Jesus," Christian whispers, looking around the packed room. "I knew she was a hoarder, but I had no idea it had gotten this bad."

It looks like something from the TV show, *Hoarders*. She never threw anything away, even garbage. And she *loved* to shop online. Not only is there a pile of clothes still in their plastic in the dining room, there's a pile of opened and empty boxes in the corner of the living room.

It's a mountain of cardboard.

"I don't want to know what's in the kitchen," Jenna says, covering her nose with her sleeve. The stench is bad enough to make your eyes water. I don't know if it's from her lying here dead for four days, or if it's from all of the garbage. "This is a gut job, you guys. Christian, if you want to get your money back from this house, you'll have to—"

"I know." He kisses her head gently. "I know, babe. Nina, is there anything here that you want to keep?"

"Have you lost your mind?"

He shrugs. "Maybe she had jewelry or something? I don't know."

"She pawned all of it." Christian's eyes widen in surprise. "I know I should have told you. She couldn't hang on to money, you know that."

"So there's nothing of sentimental value here?" Sebastian asks. I can't help but acknowledge how damn incredible the man is. We're standing in a shit hole, surrounded by blood stains from where she died, her filth, her mess, and it's as though he's not even affected by any of it.

"No," I confirm.

"Wait," Jenna says, "I saw a box in the hallway marked: *pictures*. You might want to take that."

"I'll have it shipped to Montana," Christian says with a nod. "And I'll hire a team to go through the house. Anything of sentimental value like that will be sent to us. Everything else will be donated or trashed."

Christian is carrying a small purple velvet bag that contains her remains. They're in a plastic box.

We opted out of the urn since we planned to bring her immediately here.

"Should we go outside?" he asks.

"Yes." I nod and follow him out onto the deck and down the steps to the beach below. It's nice just to breathe some fresh air. If I can help it, I'll never step foot back in that house.

We're definitely not alone on the beach, but this isn't a popular spot for recreation, especially not this early in the day, so we're not fighting any of the crowds common on the beach in southern California.

We all kick off our shoes and walk down the warm sand to where the surf kisses the shoreline.

"We're here to say goodbye to our mother, Karen Jean Wolfe," Christian begins, speaking loudly enough for us to hear him over the ocean breeze and the waves. "She was a complicated woman. I hope that after so many years of discontent, she's resting peacefully in the afterlife."

He turns to me. "Would you like to say anything?"

I look out on the horizon where a sailboat is drifting past. Do I have anything to say about my mother? I probably have too much to say. And not much of it is nice.

So I just shake my head *no* and hold onto Sebastian's hand with all my might.

Christian opens the box and shakes the ashes out onto the sand. We watch as the water washes over them, sweeping them out to sea.

And just like that, my mother is gone.

"I hate watching you struggle like this."

Sebastian's voice is a whisper in the night. We're lying in bed in Christian's house, and neither of us has slept. I feel him turn onto his side so he can watch me in the moonlight.

"Your skin is beautiful under a full moon. Have I ever told you that?"

"I don't think so." I turn to face him. We're hugging our pillows, watching each other. Only our legs touch, tangled together under the covers. "Thank you for everything you've done for me over the past couple of days."

"I haven't done *anything*." I hear the frustration in his voice. "All I've done is be with you, but I haven't been able to help you feel better, or solve anything."

"There's nothing to solve." I offer him a small smile. "And you being here is the best thing you could do for me. I would have been an even bigger mess without you."

He reaches out and drags his fingertips down my cheek. "You still look like you're torturing yourself. Her death wasn't your fault, Nina. The doctor said so himself."

"I know. But I still feel guilty."

"Why?"

"Because we stood out there today and dumped her ashes into the ocean, and I couldn't even come up with *one* nice thing to say about her. Not one, Sebastian. I should have said something in that moment. I regret not doing it."

He pulls back, stands up from the bed, and pulls me up with him. "Then let's go."

"What?"

He pulls on some pants and a T-shirt and then tosses the sundress I wore earlier at me. "Let's go back so you can say something."

"It's three in the morning."

"So?"

I blink at him. "So...we'll have to wake up Nick and Liam. That doesn't seem fair."

"They make a bleeding fuck ton of money to go where and when I tell them to, darling. Trust me, they'll be fine."

And then he's gone, out of the guest room to knock on Liam's door.

I hear them murmuring as I pull on my dress and slip into my sandals.

"Let's go," Sebastian says when he returns.

There's not much traffic to speak of at three a.m., so getting back to Mom's house doesn't take long. We avoid walking through the house by instead walking on a path that runs beside the building and down some steps to the beach below.

Nick and Liam both carry flashlights, illuminating our way down to the water. They hang back, just as they had this morning, and wait for us.

"Go ahead," Sebastian says, holding onto my hand. "Say whatever is on your mind."

"I'm so angry at you," I begin. "For a thousand different things. For being a shitty mom, and for treating us like we were a meal ticket instead of your children. For making me feel guilty every single damn day of my life because you thought I should do more for you.

"And I'm angry at you for dying." I swallow hard. "You're going to miss so much, and I don't even know if you would have cared. I mean, your son is an Oscar-winning actor, and your daughter is a successful publicist and married a freaking *prince*, and you didn't care. Not really.

"So, yeah. I'm angry. And I'm a little sad. I wish you'd been a happier person. I wish your life had been different, and you could have been happy. So I'll just say this: I hope that wherever you are now, you're finally at peace in your own mind and in your heart, Mom. I really do wish that for you. Because you were a tortured soul, and that had to be exhausting."

I take a deep breath, pulling in the salty ocean air.

"How do you feel?" Sebastian asks.

"Better," I admit. "I should have said some of that when she was alive."

"You didn't know she'd be gone so soon," he says. He's been amazing about soothing me. Trying to calm me. Just being available to listen. "And I truly believe that what they say is true, that everything happens for a reason."

And just like that, he's pissed me right off.

There's going to be hundreds of platitudes from

strangers. I don't *want* them from Sebastian.

I'm just so *angry*.

But I don't want to snap at him because he's been *so* good to me. So swoony. So loving.

"You're quite patient with me, you know."

He smiles and kisses my forehead. It's started to rain, but it's warm and feels good.

"It's not difficult to be patient with you."

I frown. "Maybe you're a little *too* calm."

He raises a brow. "Someone has to be calm."

"What the hell does that mean?" I pull away from him, ready to have a fight. I *want* a fight. I don't care if it sounds fucked up, or that I most likely need about ten years of therapy.

Bring it on.

"That in times of crisis, someone has to stay calm," he explains.

"We've all been pretty calm, considering. And I appreciate you being nice to me."

"Darling, being nice to you isn't a chore."

"Okay, I don't know what your problem is." I pace away from him in the sand, in the dark and the rain. It's the middle of the night, and I'm starting a fight with a prince on the beach, but I don't give a shit. "I don't understand how it is that I've told you I *don't* love you, and here you are, acting like the dutiful husband."

"I *am* your bloody husband."

"I know that!"

"And I told you before, you don't control my feelings."

"Why in the world would you fall for someone you're going to divorce in the next couple of years?" I demand. "Why would you do that? We're not supposed to fall in love with each other."

"Are you saying you've fallen in love with me?" he asks.

"No," I lie, raising my chin in the air. "That's *not* what I'm saying."

"Well, I've fallen in love with *you.*"

We're breathing heavily, yelling at each other, soaked to the bone.

I'm seething.

"How dare you?" I step to him, and before I can stop myself, I slap him right across the face. "How fucking *dare* you?"

I can't stay here another second. I turn and run down the beach, running away as fast as my feet will carry me through the sand and surf. I can't see well through my tears and the darkness, but I don't care.

I need to get *away.*

I don't hear anything but the rush of the water and the blood in my ears. I glance back to see that Nick's running after me.

Not Sebastian.

Nick.

Jesus, what have I done? Why do I always ruin good things?

My lungs are burning now, but I don't care. I don't want to stop.

But I trip on something in the sand, and I fall hard, banging my chin on a piece of driftwood.

I see stars when Nick catches up with me.

"Nina?" he demands as he falls to his knees beside me and takes my shoulders in his hands. "Talk to me, are you hurt?"

I can't answer him. I can hardly see him through my tears. I manage to nod my head, but I don't know what hurts worse.

My chin, or my heart.

"Did you trip?"

I nod again. Jesus, Nina, get it together.

I feel like I've broken apart and I can't put myself back together again.

"Come here," Nick says, pulling me up into his arms, cradling me and carrying me across the beach. He starts to walk back to where I left Sebastian standing on the sand. "There, there, princess. It's going to be okay."

CHAPTER 18

Sebastian

THE STING ON my cheek is nothing compared to the bruise on my heart.

I move to run after Nina, but Nick takes off like a shot. "I've got this," he calls over his shoulder.

"Let him go," Liam says as he joins me. "You need a minute, and I can't let you out of my sight."

"She wanted a fight," I say, propping my hands on my hips and watching as she sprints out of sight. The rain is falling harder now, hiding the moon, making it difficult to see. "I've been trying to keep her calm, to help her feel better."

"She's angry," Liam agrees. "Which I think is normal when you're grieving. She just needs some time. We always cut those we love the deepest."

I nod, but inside, I'm torn apart. I'm hurt. I've never had my love tossed back in my face before as if it doesn't matter at all. As if she doesn't give a bloody damn.

But I could see the turmoil in her eyes. She's absolutely in love with me.

She's just too stubborn to admit it.

"Here they come," Liam says, and I look up. Rather than walking back, Nick is carrying her, cradling her like a child.

I don't like it.

Seeing her in another man's arms makes me want to tear Nick apart with my hands.

But she's crying, and her chin is bleeding.

"Do you need a hospital?" I ask as they approach.

"No," she says softly, still not looking at me. I move to take her from Nick, but she tightens her arms around his neck.

I've been rejected by my wife twice in the same evening.

I turn on my heel and, with the help of Liam's flashlight, make my way back to the car. Nick sets Nina in the backseat next to me, but rather than lean into me, she cowers in the corner, her arms wrapped around herself.

"Nina—"

She shakes her head, cutting off the words, so I look out my window and leave her be for the drive back to Christian's home. I don't offer to hold her hand as we walk through the house to the guest suite. I don't look her way as she moves to the bed, and I veer off to the bathroom.

I need a hot shower to chase away the cold emptiness in the pit of my stomach, and a few moments to gather my thoughts.

Being an arsehole to her now won't do either of us any good. She's hurting, and instead of coming to me for comfort the way she has over the past couple of days, she lashed out at me.

I know I shouldn't let it bother me. She didn't *mean* to hurt me. Not really.

Or, maybe she did because she's hurting, too.

I don't want to lash out at her. I just don't know *how* to approach her right now. Maybe we both just need to sleep it off and revisit it in the morning.

Once I've toweled off, I walk into the bedroom, crawl into bed, and find it empty.

With a scowl, I roll over and turn on the side-light. She's not in bed. She's not sitting in the chair by the window. I *know* she's not in the loo.

Where the hell is she?

I pull on my shorts and walk into the hall. If it weren't the dead of night, I'd yell for her, but I've had the men up enough for one evening. They need to sleep.

I pad into the kitchen. Perhaps she wanted a cuppa? There's a light on over the gas range, but no Nina.

She loves to sit out by the pool, so I walk out there, expecting to see her curled up in a chair, watching the moon on the water, now that the rain has passed.

But she's not there either.

Panic starts to set in. Where in the bloody hell could she be? I make a quick turn through the living area, and when I've still not found her, I decide to wake Liam and Nick.

As I walk down the hallway, it occurs to me that there's another guest room next to ours that's not being used. I open the door and breathe a sigh of relief when I see her curled up on the bed, on top of the covers, hugging her knees to her chest.

"Nina."

She doesn't answer so I step inside, shut the door, and cross to her. She looks so small, so fragile lying there.

"Hey, why are you in here?"

I crawl onto the bed and nudge her onto her back to look at me.

"I didn't think you wanted to talk to me." Her

voice is a hoarse whisper. Her eyes are even more swollen from crying, and her hair is a mess from the rain and all of the events of the past hour.

"You're having a hell of a night, love." I kiss her forehead and then breathe a sigh of relief when she burrows her face into my chest and clings to me. "It's okay to be angry, Nina. And it's even okay to take it out on me."

"No, it's not," she wails. "None of this is okay."

"You're torturing yourself, and I won't have that, darling."

"I'm a horrible human being," she cries. "Because I can't love you. I'm *incapable* of loving you, and you're so wonderful to me. You should leave me now before it gets any worse, and I just end up ruining you."

"Okay, now you're getting a bit dramatic."

Her head pops up, and she glares at me.

"If you were incapable of love, you wouldn't be this upset."

Doesn't she see it? Doesn't she understand that she loves deeply?

"This wasn't supposed to be how it went," she murmurs. "There wasn't supposed to be any love."

"You can't control it any more than you can control the weather. Even if you set the rules."

"I just want you to be with someone who can

reciprocate your feelings."

"Nina, you love more fiercely than most people I know. Look at how loyal you are to your brother."

"Well, of *course,* I love my brother. He's my *brother.*"

"And your friends. Jenna, Grace, and Willa. And Fallon. You're incredibly loyal to all of them. You care deeply about all of them."

She doesn't say anything, she just watches my lips as I speak.

"And my sister. Darling, you and Ellie became friends faster than I could blink. You adore her.

"The only person in this world I thought incapable of love is my father, and you proved that theory wrong, too."

"I care about all of them," she says slowly. "But it doesn't mean that I *love* them."

I lick my lips, doing my best not to lose my temper. Is she seriously this stubborn? Afraid?

"Maybe we need to go back to basics here. Why don't you define love for me?"

She scowls and turns onto her back, gazing up at the ceiling. I can see the wheels turning in her head.

"It's simple, isn't it?"

"Obviously not," I reply with a grin. "How do you define love?"

She bites her lip. "Love is when you can depend on someone to stay."

I blink, taken aback a bit by her answer. But knowing what I do about her, I shouldn't be surprised at all. Everyone in her life, aside from Christian, has left her.

She never really knew her father.

Her mother emotionally abandoned her years ago.

Her friends backed out on her regarding their business, and as far as I can tell, haven't been in touch with her since.

The friends she found in Cunningham Falls are new ones. And while I have no doubt they'll be around for the long haul, Nina has no way of knowing that for sure.

"You can't love me," she continues before I can reply, "because this is temporary. You'll eventually divorce me when an acceptable amount of time has passed, and then you'll move on with your life."

"And now it's my turn to be hacked off."

Her gaze flies to mine. "Why? It's true."

"We never said this was temporary. I *never* said I planned to divorce you."

"Why would you marry a woman you don't love if you plan to be with her forever?"

"Why would *you* marry a man you don't love?"

She rolls her eyes, but I keep going.

"I'm putting that whole theory to rest right now. I'm *not* divorcing you. Not in two years, or ten, or fifty.

"If the definition of love is someone who stays, I'm here, Nina. I'm here for all of my days. I've fallen in love with you, and I don't say those words blithely. It's not something to just toss around."

I move over her and cup her cheek. "This relationship may have started as a business arrangement, but it hasn't been that for me for a long time. Do you understand what I'm saying?"

"I think so," she whispers. "I also think you're crazy."

I laugh and rest my forehead on hers. I take my time shifting out of my shorts, and sliding her clothes from her body. Her eyes are on mine as I move between her legs and gently push inside of her. Her eyes darken, but they don't leave mine.

"You're mine, Princess Nina. *Mine.* Whether you're happy or sad or bloody angry on a beach and want to take a slap at me."

"I'm sorry for that."

"You're mine," I repeat and press my lips to hers. "I love you."

"I love you, too."

I pull up so I can stare down at her, shocked

down to my toes. "What did you say?"

"You heard me. I'm still getting used to it." She brushes her fingers through my hair. "And you're mine, too. No running off to screw ladies-in-waiting or maids or any of the other girls royalty used to bone back in the day."

"No, darling. You're the only one I want to bone."

She laughs and hitches her legs up around my hips, and then there are only sighs as I remind us both that we belong to each other, now and always.

Nina is still worn out, and I don't have the heart to wake her. Even if it is after ten in the morning. She needs her rest.

So, I gingerly untangle myself from her, slip on some swim shorts and a T-shirt, and sneak out of the bedroom, headed for the pool.

I'd like to get a dozen or so laps in before we have anything else to do today.

But when I reach the pool, Christian's sitting alone, having a quiet cup of coffee.

"Good morning," he says. "Everyone in the house is still asleep. Well, not your security guys. They've been up and about for a while."

"Are they bothering you?"

"Not at all. They don't make any noise. And I know it's important to you that they're here. I'm all for safety."

"Thank you."

I sit across from him and make my own cup of coffee. I prefer tea, but it doesn't seem to be as much of a staple in American routine as coffee is.

"Did I hear you leave in the middle of the night?" Christian asks.

"You did." I sip the hot liquid and then tell him about Nina's regret at the beach yesterday, then about me taking her back and everything that unfolded after.

When I reach the end of the story, leaving it where she finally admitted that she loves me too, he shakes his head and offers me a smile.

"That all sounds like classic Nina. She can be moody, dramatic, a bit over-the-top. She should have gone into acting with me."

"So this isn't just because she's grieving?"

"Oh, that's a big part of it, yes. She's not always like this. But her first defense is always a hard one. She'll say mean things and turn the bitch level up to about a twelve, especially if she's afraid of being hurt."

"I know that's what she was doing last night. I just haven't seen it quite like this."

"She's a lot to handle," Christian admits. "She can piss me off faster than anyone else, and she can make me go all gooey inside with just a sweet smile. At the end of the day, her heart is in the right place. She just has a hard time showing emotion. And, as you've seen, love is the hardest for her. Our mom wasn't a loving person. I guess we're lucky we didn't end up as serial killers."

"My father isn't super loving either," I confide. "But I had my mum, who is, and plenty of others around me who showed me affection. Nina didn't have that."

"Aside from me? No. And then you add the fact that her brother's famous, and she always has to wonder if people want to be with her for *her*, or because of what she can do for them."

"It seems we have that in common, as well," I reply. "Despite it being an emotionally charged night, I think it was good for us. We cleared the air and finally truly expressed how we feel about each other."

"Well, since you're married and all, I'd say it's about time you did that."

I smile at him. "We did it all backwards. But it's straightened out now, and she understands that I'm not going anywhere. She's mine."

He raises a brow. "I'm glad to hear that. I was concerned that you'd worked out some sort of stupid timeline for this arrangement."

"That was never my intention."

"Since we rarely get to have a conversation in private," he says, pouring another cup of coffee from the silver carafe, "I'd like to take this time to remind you that even with all of her quirks, she's my sister and I love her. So, if you hurt her—"

"Oh, I'm going to hurt her."

He stops and narrows his eyes at me.

"I'm a human being, and I'm going to fuck it up. Probably more than I want to admit, but I can tell you this: no one will ever love her the way I do. I will protect her, I will make her feel wanted and safe, and I'll love her the best I can. I'll never raise a hand to her in anger, and I'll ruin anyone who does. I'm not a perfect man, Christian. Neither are you. But I'd say she's lucky to have both of us in her corner."

He blinks, clearly unsure how to respond.

Finally, he sips his coffee and smiles. "I guess that's all I can ask for then, isn't it?"

"I'm sure there will be other things you think of. But for now, are we good?"

"We're good."

"Excellent. What are the plans for today?"

"We're headed home." He rubs his eyes. Fatigue is heavy there. "I wanted to leave earlier, but everyone's exhausted. There's no harm in letting them sleep. Montana isn't going anywhere."

"No, but I'm ready to go."

We turn at Nina's voice. She's padding out, rubbing her still-swollen eyes. Rather than sitting in her own chair, she climbs onto my lap and buries her face in my neck.

"Good morning, darling. Do you want some coffee?"

"Yeah. This is good for now. When are we leaving?"

"Whenever we want," Christian replies. "I think Jenna's still sleeping."

"Jenna went to get donuts," she announces as she walks through the door. "I saw you guys out here having a heart to heart and didn't want to intrude. So, I ran out for sweets."

She sets the box of baked goods on the table, opens it, and sinks her teeth into a glazed.

"We're all up now," Nina says, leaning over for a donut of her own. "And after I've eaten all of these, we can go."

"You're quite bossy, darling."

She grins. "I know."

CHAPTER 19

Nina

"**W**E DON'T HAVE enough space for everyone," I say frantically as I bustle about the kitchen, putting together a charcuterie board full of cheese, veggies and meats, crackers, fruit. Snacks.

I need to have plenty of snacks on hand.

"Only Ellie and Callum are coming," Sebastian says and steals a green olive.

"No, *not* only Ellie and Callum. They bring a whole hoard of security with them, remember? Where is everyone going to sleep? I don't have enough groceries. I don't know—"

"Whoa, calm down, love. Security will work things out with Liam. I told him to use your old place for overflow."

"Oh, right. Good thinking."

"Jenna said she'd stock the fridge over there, and here, so there's plenty for everyone to snack on. You won't tell me what's happening tomorrow night, so I assume you have that under control."

"Under control," I agree with a nod, not telling him anything else. He knows that his siblings are coming for his birthday, but I want some of it to be a surprise.

"You're worrying for nothing." He swipes a piece of cheddar cheese. "This is delicious, darling. And pretty. How did you come up with it?"

I stop and stare up at him. "Are you kidding?"

"No, why?"

"It's a charcuterie board."

"A whosy what?"

I laugh and replace the cheese and olive he just took. "It's a meat and cheese tray on steroids. How do you not know this? Surely, they have this sort of thing in England."

"I don't really pay attention," he admits.

"Well, this is all the rage in the States," I tell him. "I have a whole Pinterest board dedicated to it. That's how I discovered putting these pretty little peppers on it."

"What's a Pinterest?"

"It's a place to find things."

He shakes his head. "If you say so."

"You're playing with me. You know what all of this is."

"It's fun to tease you, darling." He glances over at Liam. "When do they arrive?"

"They should be pulling into the driveway in two minutes."

"I haven't made the boozy strawberry lemonade."

"I think it's okay if the drink isn't mixed yet when they arrive."

"I'm trying to make a good impression." I stare up at him. "I'm a *woman*. This is my home. This is what we do when we have guests."

"Fascinating." He yanks me to him and kisses me silly. Kisses me until I can't remember my own name, much less how to pronounce charcuterie.

"Are you trying to distract me?"

"Absolutely."

He grins down at me. "It might have worked."

"Good."

Liam nods at Sebastian. "They're here."

"They're here!"

I turn and run past Liam and Nick, past everyone so I can yank the door open in excitement.

"Ma'am, you can't—" Liam begins, but I cut

him off.

"Oh, yes I can." I pull the door open and squeal. "You're here!"

"Oh my God, I just love it here," Ellie says as she launches herself into my arms and gives me the biggest hug ever. I know, I don't love to hug, but I *love* seeing my sister-in-law. "The view from the air is just spectacular. Those mountains!"

"I know," I say as she moves past me to greet her brother, and I turn to Callum, who's grinning at me with the same smile as Sebastian's. "I'm so happy to see you."

"Come here." He snatches me up in a hard hug. "How are you, lovely?"

"Never better."

And it's true. I feel great. I'm in love. I have amazing homes in both Cunningham Falls *and* London.

Life's damn good.

"Harrison." I give the handsome friend of Sebastian's a kiss on the cheek. "I'm so glad you came."

"Me, too. I'm excited to see the town that Sebastian's been talking about for so long."

We follow the others into the kitchen where Ellie's already attacked the charcuterie board.

"This is *gorgeous,*" she gushes. "And *so* delicious. I'm peckish after that flight."

"Now, this view is something," Callum says as he walks to the windows to look at the lake. "I'd like to take your boat out while I'm here, if you don't mind."

"I don't mind at all," I assure him. "We have two now. Sebastian bought a little speedboat last week. Mine is a bigger ski boat."

"I'll play with them both," he says with a wink.

"I want to go out on the lake, too," Ellie chimes in.

"You don't swim well," Sebastian reminds her.

"Twenty-four," she reminds him. "And old enough to make my own decisions. But thanks, big brother."

"Aww, look at that. Five minutes in, and you're already having brother-sister spats." I laugh and add more grapes to the charcuterie board. "I'll show you around the house if you like."

"Yes, I want to see everything," Ellie says, clapping her hands. "Show us."

I take them through the house, pointing out their guest rooms where their luggage has already been delivered. Then I show them the movie theater.

"You even have a popcorn machine," Ellie says. "And M&Ms."

"All you can eat," I say with a nod. "We'll have to watch a movie in here one evening. Or TV. We can get any of the streaming services in here, along with a library of movies."

"Brilliant," Callum says.

I take them to the gaming room, where there's pool and ping-pong, and accordion doors that open to the outdoor patio. Steps lead down to the guest house, the boathouse, and the dock.

"This place is just gorgeous," Ellie says. She wraps her arm around my shoulders. "And you look happy."

"I am."

"I was sorry to hear about your mum," Callum says.

"Thank you."

Sebastian steps outside and claps his brother on the shoulder. "What should we do this evening?"

"Aren't you tired?" I ask. "The jet lag is awful. Maybe you want to nap?"

"If we nap, the jet lag will be worse," Ellie says. "Let's just go upstairs and eat that amazing food, watch the water, and catch up."

"You're my favorite sister," Sebastian says, making her laugh. "That sounds perfect to me."

"It'll give your security guys a chance to rest, as well," I say with a nod. "Let's take it easy tonight. We can take Cunningham Falls by storm to-morrow."

"So, tell me about Liam," Ellie says later that eve-ning as she and I sit on the patio, drinking boozy strawberry lemonade and watching as Callum, Har-rison, and Sebastian have a look at the new speed-boat. Liam is standing nearby, along with Callum's guard.

"He's American," I reply. "Nick knows him from the military."

I glance over at Nick, who's sitting far enough away to be out of immediate earshot. I like that he's discreet, and he values my privacy.

"He's ridiculously hot," Ellie says, still talking about Liam. "And he looks a little dangerous, too."

"I think he's supposed to look that way." Sebas-tian laughs at something Callum said, then looks up at the house, searching for me. When he sees us on the patio, he sends me a little wave.

Of course, I blow him a kiss.

"He loves you," Ellie says with a sigh. "It's written all over his ugly face."

"He's not ugly." My smile is smug. "He's not ugly in the least."

"Don't let him hear you say that. It'll only give

him a big head. Now, back to Liam."

"I don't know anything else," I say with a laugh. "If you have questions, go ask him."

"It's frowned upon to fraternize with the staff." She sighs.

"But he's not technically *your* staff," I remind her. "And he doesn't even work in London."

"That's true." She grins. "Well, aren't you the clever one?"

"Does this mean it's over between you and Alistair?"

"It was never really *on* between Alistair and me. I officially told him that I don't want to see him anymore."

"How did that go over?"

"He didn't really care. I think he was as interested in me as I was in him. My mother, however, was not happy."

"I'm sure it wasn't that bad."

"Trust me, she wasn't happy. But I feel better. I don't want to be with someone boring. I want to be with someone interesting. Exciting. Maybe a little dangerous."

"I think you should talk to Liam. Just a conversation."

"He's with Sebastian 24/7."

"That doesn't mean you can't start up a conversation. And they're not together all the time. Maybe see if you can catch him early in the morning or when Sebastian's gone to bed for the evening. And, I must say, when we're here in Montana, the guys are a lot more relaxed, especially when we're at home. They monitor a lot of stuff from camera feeds and footage in the guest house."

"They don't hover all the time?"

"A lot, but not like in London or when we're away from here. So, you'll probably be able to catch Liam when he's not with your brother."

She bites her lip, watching Liam and seeming to think it over. "I'll see what happens. It's so silly because there are times I have to stand in front of hundreds of thousands of people, and I don't get nervous. But talking to an attractive man has me completely shy."

"It's not silly, and not the same thing at all," I assure her. "So, why don't you know how to swim? I'm surprised."

"I never learned," she says with a frown. "And when I was a teenager, we were at one of our summer homes that has a pond in the pasture. I went out to get my toes wet. It was hot, and I wanted to cool off."

"Sounds reasonable."

"Well, I ended up falling in and almost drowned.

Sebastian saved me."

My eyes turn to my husband. He's *in* the boat now, watching as Callum checks out the controls.

"That's scary."

"Yeah. So, since then, I just stay away from the water. But this lake is absolutely gorgeous, and there's no harm in going out on the boat. I'm not going to be swimming, for goodness sake. I'm going to sit in the boat."

"Exactly," I agree. "And we have life preservers to wear, of course, if it makes you feel safer."

"Brilliant." She clinks her glass to mine. "Perhaps after the party, you and I will slip away and go on the lake."

"By ourselves?"

She nods, sending me a sly grin.

"Without *them*?"

"You need to live a little, Nina."

"Happy birthday, dear Sebastian...

Happy birthday to you!"

I snap a photo with my phone as Sebastian blows out the candles on the beautiful cake Maisey made. It's round, and the icing is made to look like marble with golden gilding.

It's certainly a cake made for a prince.

I opted to have a smallish gathering here at home, with the same group of friends who came to the wedding. If we'd gone out to a restaurant, there would have been security concerns, and maybe even some press.

This way, we can all relax and just enjoy each other. I had dinner catered by Ciao, the cake came from Cake Nation, of course, and Brooke even brought in huge gold and silver helium balloons.

Sebastian seems pleased. He's been all smiles, has kissed me several times, and said thank you at least three times.

I'm relieved.

Because what in the world are you supposed to do for a *prince* for his birthday?

Jenna helps me cut the cake, and once it's set out for everyone to enjoy, I walk out onto the deck to find Sebastian by himself, watching the water.

"Bailed on your party already?"

He turns to me, takes my hand, and gently pulls me to him for a hug.

"I thought I'd just grab a breath of fresh air."

"Are you enjoying yourself?"

"More than I can say." He kisses my head. "Thank you for thinking of this."

"It's just a small party with friends, but I

thought you'd enjoy it."

"I am, and the fact that you thought to invite my family as well means a lot to me."

"They were excited to come. Your parents and Frederick all had previous engagements, but they sent presents with Ellie and Callum."

"I have everything I need."

"Hey, you can't throw a party and then disappear," Jenna says, poking her head out the door. "I think Willa and Max are going to leave soon."

We go back in and spend the next hour laughing and talking with our friends. They start to leave, one couple at a time, until all that's left is the two of us and Harrison, Callum and Ellie.

Actually, Ellie's gone, too.

While the guys chat in the living room, I go in search of my sister-in-law and find her downstairs on the patio, talking with Liam.

"I came to Cunningham Falls in the summers…"

I back away, not wanting to interrupt, and mentally give Ellie a high-five.

Attagirl.

"Where'd Callum go?" I ask when I get to the top of the stairs.

"He went to make some phone calls," Sebastian replies. "I finally have you all to myself."

"It's still early. Are we so old that our friends go home before midnight?"

"It seems so," Sebastian replies as he wraps his arms around my waist from behind and kisses my neck. "Let's make it an early night, too."

"I have something for you."

"This party was my gift."

"No, this party was a *party.*" I take his hand in mine and pull him through the house to our bedroom. Sitting on the bed is a big, white box, tied with a red bow.

"Is that for me?"

"Yep." I pass it to him, and we sit on the sofa by the big windows that also look out to the lake. "Open it."

He sits for a moment, not moving. "You honestly didn't have to get me anything."

"It's your *birthday*," I remind him. "And I'm already nervous enough. What in the hell does a person buy for a man who literally has *everything?*"

He smiles and unties the ribbon, lifts the lid on the box, and then looks a bit confused.

That's okay, I would be, too.

"You got me a photo album?"

"Sort of." I toss the box aside and open the cover of the album. "I got this idea the other day when we were still in California. You see, I know or have access to pretty much anything I could want to know about you. I just have to Google it or buy a book. You don't have the same privilege."

My baby photo is the first thing he sees.

"This book is *me*. I know we're still getting to know each other in a lot of ways, and I thought this would be a fun way for you to see some of my childhood, and what brought me to you."

There are school pictures. Me on a bike. My prom photo. All kinds of things.

"This was my first job," I say with a laugh. I'm dressed in a black and white uniform, serving burgers. Then it changes into me working for Christian. There's a photo of Christian and me on the red carpet at the Oscars.

And finally, we come to a selfie of Sebastian and me. And then the last photo is a candid from our wedding day.

"It may seem silly, but I just thought—"

"This is the best present anyone's ever given me," he says, looking through it all over again. "I love it. I'll treasure it always."

"I'm glad." I feel kind of silly that he's staring at my senior photo that my mom had hanging in her bedroom. I took it out of the frame and put it in the album. "I had bad hair in high school."

"Didn't we all, darling?"

"Ha. That we did." I lean my cheek on his biceps. "Happy Birthday, Sebastian. I love you."

"I love you, too."

CHAPTER 20

Nina

T HE PARTY LAST night was a hit.

Ellie, Callum and Harrison are having a good time.

And today has been a lazy one around the house. I think the past couple of days caught up with everyone with the travel and the party last night, so I haven't seen anyone today. Which is fine. A quiet day is nice now and then.

I spent the morning brainstorming a few job ideas for myself watering flowers around the property. Now that things are calming down, it's time I get to work. I enjoy working, and being a princess doesn't change that. Now, I can choose to work in areas I'm passionate about, and maybe make a difference somehow.

I'm sitting on the deck, curled up with a good book and a fresh cup of coffee. The weather is still beautiful, not a cloud in the sky, but autumn has taken hold. You can just feel the first nip of fall in the air.

Soon, it'll be time to put the boats away for winter, and I'm sure we'll head back to London. So, for today, I'm just going to sit here and enjoy my view of the lake.

I'm not sure where Nick is. Since nothing's going on, I assume he's at the guest house, keeping an eye on me via modern technology.

Which also feels great. I'm a homebody by nature, so this is my favorite kind of day.

"What are you doing?"

I turn to find Ellie walking through the glass doors, holding a can of Coke. She looks well-rested and happy.

"Being as lazy as possible."

"That seems to be going around today," she says with a laugh. "I slept *forever.* I guess the jet lag caught up with me."

She sips her Coke and sits next to me.

"I'm not sure where the guys are," I say. "I assume your brothers are off doing something together."

"I think they ran into town for something," Ellie

says with a shrug. "Maybe coffee or something."

"Good. I know they don't get to spend a lot of time together."

"Callum and Sebastian were always super close, even though they're not as close in age as Freddy and Sebastian. I think they're just kindred spirits."

"And who are you close to?" I ask her.

"All three of my brothers, for different reasons," she says with a grin. "Being the youngest with three older brothers was a curse when I was small. I had to learn to fight back. Not because they're mean, but because they were *rough.*"

"I guess it's the same for everyone, whether they're royalty or not."

"Absolutely." She nods and sips her Coke. "I have an idea."

"Okay."

"Let's go on the boat."

I raise a brow. "Now?"

"Right now. No one's around to stop us." She gives me an evil grin. "Let's sneak out, just the two of us."

"I don't know. We might get into trouble."

"Oh, we definitely will." She stands and takes my hand, pulling me up with her. "But at the end of the day, we're the boss. Not them. Let's just go

279 | Enchanting *Sebastian*

spend some time together, you and me, without a bunch of people around to listen in."

Well, put like that, it sounds wonderful.

"Okay, let's go."

We hurry inside and change into our bathing suits, I snag the boat key from the hook by the door, and then we're off, hurrying down to the dock.

"Hurry, climb in," she says with a giggle, like a little girl who's trying to get one over on her parents.

I unhook the ropes, push away from the dock, fire up the engine, and take off across the lake. When I glance back, I see Nick sprinting out of the guest house to the dock, waving his arms.

"So much trouble," I mutter as I speed away from the house to the middle of the lake.

"Oh my God, this is brilliant!" Ellie calls, holding onto the wide-brimmed hat she threw on. She's in sunglasses, and her smile is as wide as Montana. "The breeze is perfect!"

When I've driven us a few miles away and around a bend, I slow down and let us drift.

Ellie and I are both sitting in the bow of the boat, soaking up some sun.

"Now, this is the life," Ellie says with a sigh. "If I lived here, I'd be out on the boat every day."

"I usually am. I haven't been since we got back,

but before Sebastian and I came to London, I took the boat out every morning."

I glance around, realizing that there aren't many other vessels on the lake. Actually, there are *none*.

That's unusual.

"I'm so happy Sebastian met you," Ellie says, reaching over to squeeze my hand. "And that he didn't have to suffer through an arranged marriage. I can't believe that in this modern age, that's still a thing."

"I'm glad he doesn't have to be in an arranged marriage either. Honestly, I admit that I was a handful for your brother at first, but I just want to assure you that I love him very much. I couldn't be happier with him."

"It's so romantic." Ellie sighs, a dreamy smile dancing on her lips. "If you have a girl, will you name her Eleanor?"

"Uh, I haven't really given much thought to having children," I admit. In the past, I would have said, *"hell, no."* But with Sebastian? I could see it happening.

Maybe.

In quite a few years.

"Okay, enough about me." I shift in my seat so I can face her. "Tell me about your talk with Liam."

"How did you know?"

"I saw you, but I didn't eavesdrop. I regret that now. Tell me."

"It didn't last long. I asked him if he had been here before, and he said he had. He has extended family in the area. I asked him what he used to do with the military, and he said it was *classified.*"

She rolls her eyes, making me giggle.

"Did he ask you any questions?"

"He asked if he should be talking to me alone." She shakes her head. "I told him that I'm a woman, and he's a man, and if we want to have a conversation, it's not going against any laws that I know of."

"Good answer."

"And then he said he had to work and hurried off."

"Well, shit."

She sighs deeply, and I frown when a cloud moves over the sun, casting us in shadows and dropping the temperature by at least ten degrees.

The hair on my arms stands up.

"I didn't check the weather before we left," I murmur. "And I left my phone at home."

"That's not a happy cloud," Ellie says, just as raindrops start to fall. They're big, cold drops, and then, as if from out of nowhere, thunder pounds around us, and the sky opens up, dumping rain as if a tap has been opened.

"Bloody hell!" Ellie cries. We both scramble up, but we trip over each other, and in the rain, we can't see even six inches in front of our faces.

We're off balance, and the next thing I know, we're tumbling over the side of the boat into the cold, dark water below.

It's a shock to the system.

At first, I can't do anything at all, and then my arms and legs start to flail, pushing me to the surface. Just as I reach up for the rail on the boat, I hear my name being screamed.

But it's not Ellie.

"Nina!"

"Sebastian?"

"Get her out of that water!" he yells, and strong hands pull me up into the boat. I'm coughing and sputtering, trying to get the water and my hair out of my face.

I look into Nick's hard eyes. He must have jumped from the other boat into mine to pull me out. He's pissed. I don't blame him.

This was a horrible idea.

"I don't know where Ellie is!" I shout. The rain is still pounding down. I keep shoving my wet hair out of my face, but I still can't see. "She fell in, and I can't find her!"

I watch in horror as Callum and Sebastian both dive into the water. I try to wrestle out of Nick's grasp, but he growls.

"You're not going in that fucking water, Nina."

He's *never* spoken to me like that.

But, frankly, I deserve it.

I hear helicopters overhead. Liam's talking into a phone, then yells over at Nick, "They can't see anything or fly well in this weather, so they're turning around."

Nick nods, and we watch as Callum surfaces with Ellie. Callum boosts her up to Nick, who pulls her into the boat. She's sputtering and coughing, but she's breathing, and that's all that matters.

Callum joins us and hugs his sister, and my eyes are pinned to the water.

No Sebastian.

"Where is he?" I demand.

"He was with me," Callum yells back to be heard over the rain. "He passed Ellie off to me."

"Someone find him!"

"I'm going in," Liam yells before diving through the surface.

"Watch this one," Nick instructs Callum, and he joins Liam in the water.

A few seconds feels like *years*.

Where are they?

Where is my husband?

My God, if I lose him now, I don't know what I'll do. I can't. I *can't* lose him!

"There," Ellie yells, pointing as Liam and Nick surface with Sebastian, but he's unconscious. Callum's security pulls Sebastian into the other boat, and before anyone can tell me not to, I jump from my craft to the other one and ignore the look of horror Nick sends me.

I don't care.

Liam's doing chest compressions on Sebastian, and finally, Sebastian starts to cough. They turn him on his side and pound on his back, and when he sits up, his eyes find mine in the rain, which has slowed down.

But there's still thunder and lightning.

This is the *wrong* place to be in a storm.

But all I can think about is how I almost lost the love of my life.

"You jerk!" I fall on my knees next to him and pound my fists on his chest. "You said you'd never leave me! You promised. And then you almost drowned on me."

He tugs me down into his arms, hugging me close as the boat starts to move, and people yell around us, but I can't hear them. All I can focus on is Sebastian murmuring in my ear, and then his heart pounding fast against my ear as he holds me close.

"I'm here," he says, rocking us back and forth. "I'm not going anywhere."

"I've never been so scared."

"That makes two of us," he says. I can hear the edge in his voice. He's mad, too. But as long as he's alive, I don't care if he's angry. I can apologize. I can make it right.

We arrive at the house, and we're rushed inside where Jenna and Christian and Brad and Hannah are waiting with blankets, towels, and hot drinks for everyone.

How did they get here so quickly?

Harrison speaks rapidly into his phone. I assume he's talking to the palace.

"You're practically naked," Christian says in disgust as he wraps me in a towel and then jerks me into his arms. "You fucking scared ten years off my life."

"There was no storm in sight when we left." My teeth are chattering. I can't stop looking for Sebastian, and I find him standing in the living room, a blanket wrapped around him, facing the windows and watching the storm rage.

Ellie and Nick must have pulled in right behind us because they're here, too, wrapped up and glassy-eyed.

Nick glares at me.

"I'm sorry," I say to him. "I'm *so* sorry. It won't happen again."

"You're damn right, it won't happen again." Liam rushes into the room, pushing away the offer of a towel. "Now that I have search and rescue on stand-down, and I've briefed Brad and the mother-fucking *king*, you're going to tell me what, exactly, the two of you were thinking."

Ellie speaks first. "It was my idea."

"No." I shake my head. "It's my boat. My responsibility. Ellie and I decided to go out on the lake for a while."

"Then you tell Nick, and we send a team with you," Liam says. I've never seen his handsome face so hard, his expression so damn angry.

"That's the point," Ellie says, raising her chin. "We didn't *want* a whole group of people. We just wanted some time alone."

"That's not how this works, princess," Liam sneers. "And you, of all people, should know better. You have a security detail to keep you *alive*. If we hadn't installed the tracking device in Nina's boat, you would be dead right now."

Ellie pales but keeps her chin firm. "I'm not a

bloody child! I can decide if I want to go out on a stupid boat and who I want to go with. You may be the head of security, but you're not *my* boss, don't forget that."

Sebastian steps in.

"That's enough," he says.

"I've just started," Liam argues, but Sebastian shakes his head and lays his hand on Liam's shoulder.

"I know it scared you. It scared all of us. And pissed us off, as well. But yelling and belittling them isn't going to solve it."

"I resign," Liam says, shocking all of us. "I can't work like this, not if you're working against me. I can't keep you alive."

And with that, he turns on his heel and walks out.

"I'll talk to him," Nick says.

"Let him cool off first," Callum suggests. "I've never seen a man as scared as he was. And not just because his job may have been on the line, but because of the whole situation. You cocked this up, girls."

God, did we ever.

"Nina," Sebastian says. "I'd like a word privately, please."

And this is it. This is where he tells me that he

just can't deal with my shit and that it's over.

I wouldn't blame him.

I almost killed both him and his sister today.

But what will I do without him?

CHAPTER 21

I DON'T THINK I'll ever stop shaking.

Seeing Nina in that water, not knowing where Ellie was…all of it was a horror I wouldn't wish on my worst enemy.

"I don't know," I begin once I've led my wife into our bedroom and shut the door, "if I'll ever get the image of you holding onto the boat in the pouring rain out of my head. You were reckless, Nina."

"I'm sorry," she whispers and wipes a tear from her cheek. Her hair is still wet, her face still pale. "I thought I'd lost you. I'm still afraid I'm going to lose you."

"What were you thinking?"

"Ellie wanted to go out on the boat, and we really did love the idea of being alone for just a little while. But I was stupid and didn't check the weather before I got swept up into the fun of it all, and we snuck off."

"You *can't* go without security."

"I know."

"Nick may never recover."

She swallows hard. "I'll apologize again. I swear to you, Sebastian, this will *never* happen again. It was foolish."

"It was selfish."

She nods. "So, is it over, then?"

I narrow my eyes on her. "Is what over?"

"This. Us." Her lower lip quivers. "I know I fucked up big time, and I almost killed your sister today, so if you need to call this quits, I understand."

I push my hand through my wet hair and pace away from her, then back again.

"Why does your mind always go to this? You messed up, but we'll get past it, Nina."

"Oh, thank God."

I pull her to me, and she clings as if I'm the lifeline to everything good in her life.

"You said on the boat that I swore I wouldn't leave, that I *can't* leave. But damn it, Nina, you can't leave either. You can't go off like you did today and not tell anyone where you are. I was scared shitless. Liam immediately called out search and rescue, I called Brad and Christian, and then we were in the boat, racing to where the sonar said your boat was. But then the storm hit."

"That storm was ridiculous," she whispers. "It happened so fast. One minute, it was sunny and warm, and we were talking about boys and laughing. And then the next, it was a downpour, and we were in the water. I don't even know how it happened. I would *never* put your sister at risk, Sebastian. You have to know that."

"I know." I rub her back in large, slow circles, trying to calm us both down.

"And now Liam's quit. And he's so *good*, Sebastian."

"I'll make sure he stays," I assure her, but I have no idea how I'll manage it. He was livid. Terrified. As if he were reliving something from his past. A nightmare.

"Just don't send me away."

I've never heard her voice quiver with so much emotion before. I carry her to the bed and unwrap the blanket she's folded up in. Christian was right, she's practically naked in just a small bikini. It's a wonder she didn't die from hypothermia.

"So cold," she mutters, and I quickly strip out of my wet things and join her on the bed, pulling the covers over us and tugging her close to me.

"The only way I'll send you away is if I go with you." Her lips are cold against mine. She wraps one leg up around my hip, and my hand glides down her stomach to her core, to her clit. "I'm so in love with you, I can't see straight. Don't ever scare me like that again."

I push her onto her back and when I'm sure she's ready for me, I push inside her, needing to be as close to her as possible. To know that we're both alive and whole. As I thrust in and out of her, blood rushes into her cheeks, her eyes brighten, and I know she's back and that everything's going to be okay.

Her hips buck, meeting me thrust for thrust. Finally, we cry out as the wave of climax rushes over us, pulling us under.

"I need a word."

I'm standing in the guest house on the threshold of Liam's bedroom where he's currently packing his things.

"My decision is final."

I walk in and sit on the edge of his bed, bracing my elbows on my legs so I can watch him.

"I'm asking you to reconsider."

He shakes his dark head, moving faster to fill his suitcase.

"Liam, you're the best man I have, and that's saying a lot."

"You almost fucking *died* today because those women can't follow simple instructions. Because they thought it would be *cute* to try and get away with something. I refuse to have any more deaths on my watch. I won't do it."

"Liam, you did everything right today. And you saved my life, which is *exactly* your job. You saved my sister. I'm grateful. And I think everyone learned a valuable lesson today. It won't happen again."

He sighs and braces his hands on his hips. "I should be fired for insubordination."

"You should," I agree and smile when his brown eyes fly to mine. "But I won't fire you because they deserved the dressing down, and it showed me that you care about more than just the paycheck."

"It's a fucking fault of mine."

"I don't see it that way. You're protecting my family, and I want you to care about the people you work for. It shows integrity and ethics."

He sighs now, and I feel a weight lift off my shoulders because I know he's going to accept my offer to stay.

Thank God.

"I'll raise your pay."

"I don't need more money," he says. "I need the family to work with us instead of against us. It wasn't just me today. It was Nick and every other man on staff, as well."

"I understand that."

"How are they?" he asks. "How are the princesses?"

"Exhausted. Shook up. But they'll be okay, thanks to you."

He exhales.

"Please stay, Liam."

"I'll stay." He nods once. "On the condition that the crown doesn't interfere with my work."

"Understood. Thank you."

I shake his hand, surprised to feel it still trembling. Yes, something happened in Liam's past that led to this reaction. I won't ask him to explain.

Not today.

"Ma'am, you can't go in there!"

Callum and I stare at each other in response to the scuffle outside the front door. "What's going on?" he asks.

"I have no bloody idea."

We stomp to the front door, right behind Liam, who opens it. I'm surprised to see a woman with a riot of curly, red hair, her arms laden with bags, struggling with the security Liam has posted at the door.

"Release her," I command. They both immediately let go of her arms. "What's this about?"

"Hey." She blows her hair out of her face. "This is like Fort Knox."

"Maybe better," Callum says and leans his shoulder against the door, crossing his arms over his chest and sending her a charming smile. "What's your name, darling?"

"I'm Aspen Calhoun," she says. "I heard about the emergency y'all had yesterday, and I thought I'd bring some coffee and pastries this morning. Oh, I'm the new owner of Drips & Sips."

"Come in." I glance back at Liam, who nods, and I gesture for Aspen to follow me into the house. I lead her to the kitchen where she sets the bags on the counter.

"You're from the café," Nina says as she walks into the room. She looks fresh and well-rested this morning, as if the events of yesterday afternoon didn't happen. But I know she was up half the night with nightmares.

"I am," Aspen says with a smile, and then she

gets a good look at Nina, then me, and Christian sitting in a chair by the window. Her jaw drops. "No wonder you have good security. I just walked into Hollywood."

"You didn't know?" Nina asks as she helps Aspen unload her bags.

"No. There was some gossip in Drips yesterday afternoon because the search and rescue guys came in for coffee. They said it was you, and I knew you married a prince, but I honestly didn't connect the dots. I've been so busy with this new business, I barely remember my own name.

"But I've been through the search and rescue thing before, and it's so dang exhausting. I just thought it would be nice to not have to worry about breakfast."

"Thank you," Jenna says with a smile. "And, please, tell us more about buying Drips. We were afraid the new owner would change everything."

I take a huckleberry scone and bite into it, enjoying the conversation.

"I'm not changing *anything*," Aspen assures the girls. "I've worked there as a barista for about a year now, and I love it. The staff is great, the customers are fun. I might add some food items for lunch, but that's all."

"What made you decide to buy it?" Nina asks.

"It's time I fit in somewhere," Aspen murmurs

and then pastes a smile on her pretty face. I glance up to find Callum watching her thoughtfully as he sips his coffee.

I know that look.

Callum thinks she's hot.

"It made sense," Aspen continues. "Anyway, I don't want to take up any more of your time. I hope you enjoy."

"Thank you so much," Nina says with a smile and a wave as Liam walks Aspen to the front door. "I'm so glad someone nice bought it."

"Me, too," Jenna agrees, reaching for a second scone.

"What did I miss?" Ellie asks as she walks into the room.

"Food," Callum says before rushing off to catch up with Aspen.

Ellie raises an eyebrow. "Was there a girl?"

"A pretty one," Nina affirms. "Aspen Calhoun."

"Irish," Ellie says as she reaches for a scone. "Did she have red hair?"

"As a matter of fact, she does," Jenna says.

"Callum's always had a thing for redheads," Ellie says. "Isn't that right, Sebastian?"

"I wouldn't know."

Ellie rolls her eyes. "Yes, you do."

"I know that I have a thing for this blonde right here." I kiss the top of Nina's head. She cranes her neck back so she can smile up at me.

"That's a good answer."

CHAPTER 22

Nina

One Year Later

"INTRODUCING, HIS ROYAL HIGHNESS, the Duke of Somerset, Prince Sebastian. And Her Royal Highness, the Duchess of Somerset, Princess Nina."

Sebastian and I enter the room to a round of applause. We're dressed to the nines, as fancy as it gets, for this state dinner. Just a year ago, I would have been completely sick to my stomach with nerves.

But after a full year of being married to Sebastian, I can honestly say that I look forward to getting all dressed up in pretty gowns with gloves up to my elbows and dripping in jewelry. I mean, doesn't every little girl dream of dates like this one? I have a handsome prince on my arm, and I'm in a room with some of the most powerful men and women in the world.

But the very best part is the reason everyone is assembled here this evening. My charity, *Her*, is finally up and running. We're working tirelessly to help women in all of the commonwealth countries to escape abuse.

No woman should ever be harmed, especially from someone they love.

I've worked my ass off to get it off the ground, and we're finally here.

Not only do the king and queen support it, they insisted on this amazing state dinner to celebrate, inviting nobility from all over Europe to attend, and to donate to the cause.

Sebastian and I sit at the table, directly across from each other. I'm sandwiched between the Queen of Denmark and the Prime Minister of France.

Nick stands discreetly behind me in case an assassin storms the castle and decides to threaten my life.

Honestly? It makes me feel better to know he's there. Since the horrible scene on the lake last fall, I've followed the security detail's instructions to the letter, and there hasn't been another incident since that one.

I still feel guilty about it.

Sebastian smiles at me from across the table as the Prime Minister of Canada's wife talks his ear off.

It's funny, really. He's a handsome and charming man. Women like to talk with him.

But only *I* get to go home with him later.

Maybe I'll take his pants off with my teeth. It seems like an ambitious endeavor, but it would surprise him, and I'm all for that.

Liam is with us on this trip to London. Charles had a family emergency, so Liam's with Sebastian, and I think my husband prefers it that way. Not that he doesn't love Charles, but the man is nearing retirement age.

Liam's eyes dart to my right and narrow. I follow his gaze and smile when I see he's looking at Ellie. She's flirting with the young gentleman sitting next to her, and I can see that Liam doesn't like it one bit.

The evening is uneventful and full of small talk. When Sebastian and I finally make our way to our apartment, I'm nervous and excited all at the same time.

"That was amazing," he says as he loosens his tie. "I've never been more proud of you than I was during your incredible speech. You had some of the world's most powerful people in tears today."

"I'm passionate about this cause, and I want it to do well."

"It's going to be a smashing success. You're changing lives, Nina."

I smile at my husband's praise. He's been my biggest supporter.

"It was lovely that your parents insisted on tonight's event. I think we'll have some impressive donations roll in from it. Not to mention, your father was charming this evening."

"He's partial to you." He leans in and kisses me in that way he does that always makes my world tilt on its axis.

"I have something I want to talk to you about," I begin and bite my lip. I haven't even stepped out of my shoes yet, I'm so nervous.

"Okay." He frowns. "Are you all right?"

"Oh, yeah. I'm fine." I swallow hard and pray he won't be mad. Or weirded out. "We just haven't talked about this before."

"Just spit it out."

"I was thinking of having my IUD removed so we could maybe have a baby."

I watch as a myriad of emotions make their way across his handsome face. Confusion, disbelief, and then pure joy.

"Yes, I'm absolutely on board with that."

"Oh, thank goodness. I thought maybe you didn't want kids."

"I want children. Of course, I do. I just didn't want to bring it up because I thought it was something you didn't want."

"I never did," I admit and finally kick the heels off my feet. "Until you. And now I can't imagine *not* having children with you. You'll be a wonderful father."

His kiss is long and slow. Incredibly romantic.

Is it possible to get pregnant from just a kiss? Because if so, I'm pretty sure I'm having triplets.

"Let's get started right now," he says.

"I still have to go to the doctor and have the stupid thing removed," I remind him with a laugh.

"We can practice, can't we?" He tugs me toward the bedroom, but there's a knock at the door. "Bloody interruptions."

"They want the jewelry back," I remind him as I open the door. The man in charge of the crown jewels collects the tiara, necklace, and earrings, and then he's gone. "It always makes me nervous, wearing several million dollars in jewelry on my body."

"It suits you," he says simply. Just as he retakes my hand, there's another knock on the door. "Now, I'm going to kill someone."

But when he opens the door, it's Liam. "The plane will be ready at six in the morning, sir."

"Excellent."

He shuts the door and turns back to me.

"If anyone else knocks, we're ignoring it."

"Where are we going tomorrow?"

"It's a surprise."

"Tell me."

He laughs and tosses me onto the bed. "You really need to get better at surprises, darling."

"Just give me a hint."

"No. I still wear the pants in this family."

I cock a brow and lean over to tug his pants free with my teeth. Once I get them down his legs and toss them aside, I smile triumphantly.

"You're not wearing pants now."

"Well, that was fun."

"I have more fun things up my sleeve."

"Oh, darling, I'm counting on it."

EPILOGUE

PRINCESS ELEANOR ROSE Elizabeth Wakefield.

Princess.

All anyone ever sees is the princess, not the woman behind the title.

There's a lot about being a part of the royal family that I love. Of course, I love my actual family, but I also enjoy the comforts and privileges that come with the title. I won't deny it.

But there's also quite a lot that's expected of me that feels stifling.

Saying *"not a chance in bloody hell"* to the proposal by one Beauregard Hattenham was exactly the *opposite* of what my parents expected.

He's handsome.

And he's an earl, so he has an appropriate bloodline.

He's got an education from an Ivy League institution.

His family's wealthy.

On paper, he looks perfect for the youngest daughter of a king.

In person? He's an arsehole. I'd rather marry Alistair, the most boring and slobbery man on Earth.

None of the men my parents seem hell-bent on parading in front of me are marriage-worthy. Why are Mum and Father suddenly so obsessed over whether or not I find a suitable husband? I'm only twenty-five, for God's sake. It's not like I'm an old maid.

So, I left. I didn't tell anyone except my security team and the pilot of the plane. I didn't even call ahead to ask if I could barge in on Sebastian and Nina in Montana.

I just decided to show up.

At two in the morning.

No big deal.

The journey in the car from the airport to the house takes less than fifteen minutes. We walk up to the front door, and before I can knock, it opens.

I expect to see my brother.

Instead, it's Liam, frowning down at me.

I didn't expect to see him, but here he is in all of his scowling, disapproving, more handsome than sin glory.

"Hello, princess."

About Kristen Proby

Kristen was born and raised in a small resort town in her beloved Montana. In her mid-twenties, she decided to stretch her wings and move to the Pacific Northwest, where she made her home for more than a dozen years.

During that time, Kristen wrote many romance novels and joined organizations such as RWA and other small writing groups. She spent countless hours in workshops, and more mornings than she can count up before the dawn so she could write before going to work. She submitted many manuscripts to agents and editors alike, but was always told no. In the summer of 2012, the self-publishing scene was new and thriving, and Kristen had one goal: to publish just one book. It was something she longed to cross off of her bucket list.

Not only did she publish one book, she's since published more than thirty titles, many of which have hit the USA Today, New York Times and Wall Street Journal Bestsellers lists. She continues to self publish, best known for her With Me In Seattle and Boudreaux series, and is also proud to work with William Morrow, a division of HarperCollins, with the Fusion and Romancing Manhattan Series.

Kristen and her husband, John, make their home in her hometown of Whitefish, Montana with their adorable pug and two cats.

Website
www.kristenproby.com

Facebook
www.facebook.com/BooksByKristenProby

Twitter
twitter.com/Handbagjunkie

Goodreads
goodreads.com/author/show/6550037.Kristen_Proby

Other Books by Kristen Proby

Coming Soon
Shadows: A Bayou Magic Novel

The Big Sky Series
Charming Hannah
Kissing Jenna
Waiting for Willa

Kristen Proby's Crossover Collection – A Big Sky Novel
Soaring with Fallon
Wicked Force: A Wicked Horse Vegas/Big Sky Novella by Sawyer Bennett
All Stars Fall: A Seaside Pictures/Big Sky Novella by Rachel Van Dyken
Hold On: A Play On/Big Sky Novella by Samantha Young
Worth Fighting For: A Warrior Fight Club/Big Sky Novella by Laura Kaye
Crazy Imperfect Love: A Dirty Dicks/Big Sky Novella by K.L. Grayson
Nothing Without You: A Forever Yours/Big Sky Novella by Monica Murphy

The Fusion Series
Listen To Me
Close To You
Blush For Me
The Beauty of Us
Savor You

The Boudreaux Series
Easy Love
Easy with You
Easy Charm
Easy Melody
Easy Kisses
Easy Magic
Easy Fortune
Easy Nights

The With Me In Seattle Series
Come Away With Me
Under the Mistletoe With Me
Fight With Me
Play With Me
Rock With Me
Safe With Me
Tied With Me
Burn With Me
Breathe With Me
Forever With Me
Stay With Me
Indulge With Me
Love With Me
Dance With Me

The Love Under the Big Sky Series
Loving Cara
Seducing Lauren
Falling For Jillian
Saving Grace

From 1001 Dark Nights
Easy With You
Easy For Keeps
No Reservations
Tempting Brooke
Wonder With Me - Coming Soon!

The Romancing Manhattan Series
All the Way
All it Takes

CPSIA information can be obtained
at www.ICGtesting.com
Printed in the USA
LVHW091235290919
632570LV00006B/46/P

9 781633 500488